As soon as s

nightclothes, a vi

slumped to the floor.

Glass shattered somewhere in the distance, and a man's gloved hand breached the gaping hole of the French door pane, disengaging the bolt.

The door swung open, hinges creaked, and the killer stepped inside, dressed in black. He carefully made his way into the living room.

He crept around to the kitchen with a knife clutched in his hand. Jenna's breath caught the moment she realized the room he peered into was the same as the one belonging to the rental house.

Oh my God, is he in here?

Fear rained down on her. As much as she struggled to move, nothing happened, and it was a horrifying reality knowing until this vision played out, she wouldn't be able to. *He's going to kill me right here while I'm helpless, and I can't do anything about it. Please, somebody, help me*

He turned into the hallway.

Now approaching the guest bedroom.

The killer stopped and peeked inside, then skulked past the bathroom, moving to her bedroom at the end of the hall.

In another minute he would be at her door.

Praise for Donnette Smith

"Mrs. Smith is an author to be reckoned with."

~Jack Strandburg

"Cunja is a mysterious, graphic, paranormal, fantasy horror that James Patterson himself would be proud of."

~Oya Pearl

"Donnette is a master storyteller. Her writing style is crisp and refreshing and I look forward to her next book!"

~T.G.Reaper

"Mrs. Smith has found her calling.... I found myself NOT wanting to put this down."

~Linda Barbane

"The author has done a fabulous job of meshing a truly terrifying idea with the well-known and still respected ghosts of New Orleans. It was an honor to read Cunja, and it is a story I will definitely read again."

~Night Owl Reviews

Killing Dreams

by

Donnette Smith

Killing Dreams

Contact Information: info@thewildrosepress.com

Cover Art by *Kristian Norris*

The Wild Rose Press, Inc.
PO Box 708
Adams Basin, NY 14410-0708
Visit us at www.thewildrosepress.com

Publishing History
First Edition, 2021
Trade Paperback ISBN 978-1-5092-3821-7
Digital ISBN 978-1-5092-3822-4

Published in the United States of America

Dedication

Thank you, Mom, for tearing my original manuscript to shreds. Your honesty at times drove me to madness, but it pushed me to work harder, to reach into my soul and rewrite, and rewrite some more. By the time I sent you the third draft, I was on the verge of giving up. But what was it you said to me? "My daughter, now you're writing." You were hard when you needed to be and gave me praise only when I earned it.

Lindsey Snyder, a big thank you for willing to be my beta reader. You were behind the scenes as my copilot, always sending me your thoughts. Your constant words of encouragement gave me just the push I needed to finish the manuscript.

My husband, Allen, of thirty-two years is the inspiration for every male hero that comes across the pages of my books. Thank you for being my knight in shining armor and for the unconditional love you have shown me since the day you stole my heart.

And to my father. Dad, I miss you more than the earth misses the sun on a winter day. If heaven has guitars, I know you are singing to the angels.

Chapter One

Jenna Langley screamed, then opened her eyes. The room slowly came into focus. In the darkness, shadows played deceptive tricks. After the place she visited tonight, and the horrible thing that happened there, she half expected something to lunge toward her as she lay in an immobile state, helpless.

If she could just move.

It was no use. The loss of function she experienced now was the same as when it happened before. No one was around to wake her, to make the nightmare stop. She prayed to God the killer she saw while spirit walking couldn't find her here, alone in the dark.

Something crashed outside the house. The French door burst open. Curtains blew inward. An unidentified object shifted across the patio.

With a sharp intake of breath, she sat up in bed, thankful the ability to move had returned. Trembling, she fumbled for the lamp on the bedside table. She needed to get up quickly.

He was coming.

Glass shattered on the floor.

She managed to turn on the light and stared beyond the opened doors. Lightning flashed in the sky, an omen of a coming storm. Thank God. The wind caused the noise outside.

But it did nothing to calm her nerves. The remnants

of the out-of-body experience still clung in the vision of the brutal murder—and the man who committed it. The face of the young woman who fought so hard to hold on to life, only to have it ripped away, would stay with Jenna for a very long time.

As she stepped on the floor, something pricked her foot. Broken glass covered the white carpet. Damn, the cup on the nightstand must have gotten knocked over when she turned on the lamp. Inspecting her foot, she found a small sliver embedded in the sole.

After limping to the bathroom, she did her best to remove the shard, but her hands continued to shake like a leaf in the wind. Her mind was still hazy, as if she'd been drugged. But the same thing had occurred after the last spirit walk, hadn't it? After all these years, it was amazing she still remembered it. Until tonight, she'd chalked the phenomenon off to a teenage memory.

Now they were occurring all over again.

Yet, this one was different. She'd witnessed a murder, and God if it wasn't real as hell. The way the man strangled the life out of that girl. How she'd clawed at his hands, twisting, and bucking. Tears formed in her eyes at the memory. Nightmares? They might be vivid—but not like this.

She considered picking up the phone and calling her mother. But the comfort of those actions would come with a heavy price. Amanda Langley would warn these experiences were happening again because of her poor choice to return to Texas, to the place where it all began. Although Jenna had no idea of the time, getting her mom involved would be stupid even though the ever-heightening anxiety almost drove her to that point. She was an adult, for crying out loud. It was time to start acting like one.

After tending to her foot, she hobbled back to the bedroom. Stepping out on the patio to inspect for any storm damage was not an option. With her imagination running wild, she pictured the crazy maniac who killed that girl tonight waiting just outside the door. Instead, she shut and locked the doors and snapped the curtains shut, too afraid to take even one glance out the windowpane. She was sticky from sweat and needed a shower but was way too spooked to climb into one while alone in a strange place. She'd seen that movie, thank you very much.

Still shaken, she searched through the house, turning on every light, checking to make sure all the locks were secured. After going back to the bedroom, she grabbed the remote and flipped on the television, hoping the sound would distract her from this unexplainable fear.

One look at the clock told her it was barely five a.m. She had three hours to kill before she was scheduled to arrive at the new client's place of business. That much time might as well be an eternity. Something to get her mind off the terror she'd experienced tonight would be just the thing. Then an idea occurred. When she rented this place two weeks ago, she'd found a pack of cigarettes and lighter in one of the kitchen cabinets. Either the landlord or one of his tenants had been a smoker. But she shouldn't. Giving up smoking a year ago had been a really hard thing to do. On the other hand, a quick smoke would calm her nerves.

Mind made up, she headed to the kitchen and retrieved the cigarettes and lighter. The pack was already open with a few missing, and probably stale as hell, but she didn't care.

She carried the lighter, a makeshift ashtray, and cigarettes over to the kitchen table, set them down, and drew out a chair. Sitting, she considered her lease agreement. No smoking inside the house. Well, screw it. The homeowner can keep the deposit. Paying for carpet and drapery cleaning was better than stepping foot outside that door in the dark.

Lighting the cigarette, she wondered what caused the out-of-body experiences to start up again. The last time she'd been sixteen, but even then, no one died. Hell, she was never certain they were even real. What if it was a figment of her imagination? Perhaps she had a brain tumor all these years and didn't even know it. No, her parents were religious about routine health checks. But what about a CT scan?

She needed to stop this insanity. There was nothing wrong with her. Bad dreams were a part of life. People got them all the time. She took a deep breath and stubbed out the cigarette. The rational thing to do would be to give it time and see what happened before jumping to conclusions.

Now that Jenna managed to calm her nerves, she began to consider taking a shower once more. It would certainly keep her mind off the nightmare and help to pass the time.

She grabbed the cigarettes and tossed them into the trash on the way to the bathroom. Her daughter was right. Smoking was a nasty habit.

****

Jenna sat at the bar inside the Texas Roadhouse, sipping a margarita and waiting for Barbara Cassidy to arrive. It had been good to see an old friend when they ran into each other at the grocery store. Since coming back to Texas after ten long years, she had yet to feel at home. Given her history, and what happened before leaving, it was doubtful such a thing could even be possible.

It didn't matter. She wasn't here to relive the past. Business brought her to the Lone Star state this time. And she'd be damned if the memories of a teenage breakup would ruin things. Not after all this time.

The sound of shattering glass sent a wave of panic reeling through her.

At the immediate response of "Sorry! My bad" coming from behind the bar, she closed her eyes and sighed.

The place was packed for a Tuesday night, leaving no other option than to take a seat at the bar. Between the racket of guests and staff shuffling about, and that damn neon sign blinking above her head, she felt like she was going nuts. Though it had been three days since her out-of-body experience, images of that night still lingered. If Barbara knew she'd slept with the lights on since then, she would get a good laugh for sure.

Someone clapped her on the back, and she jumped.

"On edge these days, huh?" Barbara asked, sliding into the stool beside her.

Just then a lady walking past lost her balance, bumped into Jenna and splashed most of her drink down her shoulder. The woman who appeared so tipsy she didn't realize her misstep went on her merry way.

"You have no idea," she answered, grabbing a tissue from the bar to dab the liquid soaking through the material of her dress.

"Really?"

"Don't look so intrigued."

"Well, you know me."

In school, Barbara was the inquisitive one. Always knew everyone's business. But she had been one of those friends that had your back, no matter what. And that was what Jenna remembered the most about her.

Barbara ordered a drink. "So, are you going to tell me?" She grabbed a few peanuts from the small, metal bucket, cracked them open, and threw the peanut shells on the ground, as was customary for guests at the Texas Roadhouse.

"Tell you what?"

"What's got you so on edge?" she said, tossing a few nuts in her mouth.

"Oh, that." She picked up the drink and took a swallow. "It's nothing."

Her friend snorted. "Since when has that ever worked on me?"

"Okay. Do you remember when I was having those out-of-body experiences as a kid?"

"I think so." She peered upward in thought. "Yes, actually I do. As I recall they freaked you out. But you stopped having them, didn't you?"

"I had one a few nights ago. It was really disturbing."

"Disturbing, how?"

Seeing that expression in Barbara's eyes reminded Jenna of old times. Until now, she hadn't realized how much she'd missed her best friend's company. "I saw a girl being murdered. I swear, it was so real."

The bartender set Barbara's martini down. Her friend slid the olive into her mouth, chewed, then took a sip. "Maybe it was a nightmare."

"You're probably right. I just haven't been able to get my mind right since."

"That's why I'm here."

Jenna grinned, recalling Barbara's talent for getting someone in a better mood. Sometimes, what she wouldn't give to go back to her teenage years. Then the memory of Cole Rainwater surfaced, and the grin vanished.

As if in sync with her thoughts, her friend asked, "Have you seen Cole yet?"

Despite all good intentions, Jenna's pulse spiked at the mention of his name. "No. And I don't plan to."

"He still lives in Farmersville, you know."

She shrugged, giving the impression it didn't matter. But inside a storm brewed and denying she hadn't stopped thinking about him since her plane touched down in Texas seemed pointless.

"Where are you staying while you're here?"

Her mind drew a blank.

Barb waved a hand in front of her face. "Earth to Jenna."

"Sorry." She cleared her throat. "I didn't hear what you said."

"You still think about him, don't you?"

"Hell no." Now she remembered why Barbara used to get on her nerves. The girl was too intuitive for her, and everyone else's good.

"Yes, you do. It's written all over your face."

"Still believe you know everything, huh?"

"You're not getting off that easy."

"There's no juicy insight here, Barbara. We broke it off when we were seventeen. I moved to Georgia. We both got on with our lives. End of story."

"Just so you know, he's not seriously involved with anyone." Shaking her head, her friend said, "It's quite strange."

"Because he's not married?" Neither was she.

"It's been ten years is all. You'd think he would have moved on. Ya know, settled down with someone by now."

"I haven't." She regretted the words the moment they left her lips.

"That so?"

The last thing she needed was to have her best friend scrutinizing her life and come up with justification as to why she and Cole never committed to other relationships. As if she cared. It's none of her business what that man did. She dared to stare her friend in the eyes. "I've had a few relationships. Just no one I want to get serious with, yet."

Barbara took the hint. "So why exactly are you in Texas?"

"Business. I sold my company a few years ago and went into consulting. I have a client here."

As her friend chattered on, Jenna noticed a familiar face flash across the television screen above the bar. Her breath caught. Goosebumps crawled a path up her arms as she stared into the face of the woman she'd seen in the spirit walk. She interrupted the bartender and asked him to increase the volume of the TV. Barbara quieted, as Jenna listened to the broadcast.

The photo depicted a smiling woman who was once full of life. But nothing could erase the terror she'd seen in the girl's eyes while that monster strangled the life out of her.

According to the newscast, the name of the murdered girl was Sylvia Clark and she was nineteen years old. Her burned body had been discovered in Brushy Creek in nearby Farmersville. The autopsy report listed the cause of death as strangulation. And as equally shocking, as the news reporter switched focus onto the lead detective for the Farmersville PD: Cole Rainwater.

Staring at a much older version of Cole, Jenna's mouth dropped open. His hair was slightly longer than it once was, and the contours of his face had filled out. But she would know those striking gray eyes anywhere. "Is that Cole?"

"That's him, all right," Barb chirped. "He joined the police academy a year after you left."

Jesus Christ, none of what happened during her spirit walk was an illusion. And her ex-boyfriend, the one relationship she'd never been able to completely put out of her mind, was investigating the murder. What were the chances?

She glanced at her friend. "We need to talk. Can we go to my place?"

Staring at her for a moment too long, the expression in Barbara's eyes told Jenna she was getting a little concerned. "Are you okay?"

"Not really. But I need to talk to someone."

"You all right to drive?"

"Yes."

Barbara collected her purse and slid off the stool. "I'll follow you then."

****

"Are you thirsty?" Jenna asked Barbara as they settled in at the rental.

"Sure. What have you got?" Her friend took a seat on the couch as Jenna crossed the room.

"How about Southern Comfort?"

"Oh, you have been a bad girl."

She let go of a laugh and strolled into the kitchen to get the booze. "I thought you'd like that," she hollered into the living room.

"Our favorite liquor. When was the last time we drank it?"

"It was Christmas break, 2010. A few months before I left."

"That's right," Barbara said, as Jenna sauntered back into the room, two glasses with ice cradled in one hand, and the bottle of whiskey hanging from the other. "Your folks were out of town, me, you, Cole, and Michael drank the whole bottle. We got wasted, and…"

"Michael spent the whole night throwing up," they both said in unison.

"Whatever happened to Michael?" Jenna wanted to know, laughter in her voice.

Barbara rolled her eyes. "He got all big city on us."

"What'd he do, move to New York?"

"That's exactly what he did."

"No kidding."

"He heads up some big law firm in the city."

"He always said he wasn't cut out for country life."

"I guess you weren't either."

Setting a glass down in front of her friend, Jenna's smile disappeared. She filled it halfway, poured some for herself, then trekked over to the chair across from Barbara. "Trust me, it's more complicated than that."

"I wouldn't know. You never did tell me. You broke some hearts when you left, ya know."

"It wasn't like I had a choice. I was seventeen. My parents were leaving."

"Jenna, you didn't even say goodbye to any of us. I found out from the man who owned the hardware store in town. Said he saw your parents pull up at the gas station across the street with a U-Haul."

The ceiling fan above her head spun, and in the silence, Jenna picked up the ticking of the ceramic ball at the end of the pull chain as it struck the lighted globe. "There are things you just don't know."

"Obviously. You plan on telling me?"

Jenna shook her head. "I can't."

"So, you don't trust me? I was your best friend."

Even though Jenna had been away so long, interacting with Barbara again reminded her that nothing had changed between them. Their friendship picked right back up where it left off a decade ago. But knowing Barb as well as she had, this discovery didn't surprise her.

"I know. And it's not that. It's just…complex."

Her friend picked up the drink and took a sip. "I think I know what happened."

A sudden wave of fear washed over her. There was no way Barbara could know. Nobody knew the real reason her parents left Texas except them and herself. She was sure of it.

"It's about what happened with Cole's father, right?" Barb said. "The guy was a serial killer, and none of us knew. Not even his son. You should have seen how badly your leaving affected him. Not only did he have to deal with what his dad had done, but he had to come to terms with the guy's suicide too. Man, there was a time during that year I didn't think Cole would make it through. In the middle of everything, you left, and you didn't even tell him."

Anger inflamed her cheeks. "My parents refused to let me see him after that. They kept me locked in the house. One of them was always with me. I couldn't even make a phone call. And even if I could, I doubt he would have talked to me. He didn't want to see me. I waited by the phone for a month for him to call and checked the mailbox every day hoping he'd write. If I left him so broken-hearted, why didn't he try to come see me?"

Her friend appeared nonplussed. "I don't know."

When Jenna's anger abated, she was at least relieved Barbara didn't know her secret. No one could know what she had been hiding, especially not Cole.

"Why didn't you call me?"

"God, Barbara, I was going through hell."

"All the more reason for you to have gotten in touch. I could have helped you."

"No one could help me. My parents isolated me from everyone. Then they whisked me away to Georgia."

"I'm sorry, Jenna. I just figured you didn't want anything more to do with any of us after what happened with Cole's father. If I'd have known, I would have gone to your house and told your mother to stuff it. Then I would have demanded Amanda let me see you whether she liked it or not."

"I would have liked to have seen that."

Barbara snickered. "So would I. Your mother thought I was a bad influence on you."

"You were."

Barbara grinned, picked up her half-empty glass

and took a sip. "Guess she was right about that." After clearing her throat, the seriousness on her face got Jenna's attention. "You and Cole loved each other. I was so envious because Michael and I didn't have what you guys had."

"Well, you see how that turned out. Besides," she said, taking a long swig. "It was a long time ago. We all grew up."

"So, what did you drag me here to tell me?"

"Yeah, that." This called for more alcohol. She gulped down the rest of her drink and poured another. After Barbara finished off hers, Jenna refilled the glass and took a deep breath. "The girl on the news? It's the same young woman I saw being murdered during my out-of-body experience the other night."

Her friend frowned and rolled her eyes. "How can you be sure?"

"The birthmark on her cheek, the one shaped like a strawberry, it's the same one. She had blonde hair and blue eyes. Just like the murder victim I saw."

Shaking her head, Barbara gave off a sigh. "There's got to be another explanation. Maybe the girl just resembled her."

"No, it was the same person."

Doubt shadowed Barbara's eyes. "Jenna, something like that is just not possible. You must know that, right?"

She gazed at the floor, twisting her foot back and forth, considering Barbara's words. Her friend was right. The spirit world was probably nothing more than a far-fetched fantasy, and the gifts so-called psychics claimed to have had most likely didn't exist. Even the few times Jenna experienced what she could only have described as spirit walks, it was a struggle to embrace the reality of such a thing. Although strange occurrences happened sometimes, someone shouldn't make too much of it.

But what happened a few nights ago had been so traumatic, that the face of the murdered young woman had been seared into her memory. As tempting as denying the truth had been, deep inside she realized it was the same person. "The girl on the news was strangled. So was the one I saw." Her words sounded pathetic, even to her ears. You couldn't convince someone to believe you when you scarcely believed yourself.

"I think you had a bad nightmare. And the girl resembling the one you saw in your dream is just some crazy coincidence. You should put the incident out of your mind. If it happens again, then you have reason to worry."

Hadn't she told herself the same thing a few days ago? Barbara's advice made perfect sense. "Okay," Jenna said, deciding to give it some time, and then taking a long drink.

"Atta girl."

Why didn't she feel any better though? A nagging sense that this was far from over wouldn't allow her to completely let it go.

"So, if we are going to continue this," Barbara said, lifting the glass and pointing at it, "I'll need to know if you have an extra pillow and blanket."

Jenna grinned as her friend grabbed the bottle of Southern Comfort. "Sure do."

Chapter Two

Long after Jenna climbed into bed, the strange sensation of something tugging at her again returned. She instantly recognized what was happening. *Oh, God, please, no.* She didn't think she could handle a second round.

Now, standing there and gazing down at her dormant form, she tried to step toward the bed where she laid sleeping. But something hauled her out into the direction of the French doors, onto the patio, and across the meadow.

Floating above several houses and streets, she lost all sense of direction. The wind carried her above the tops of trees, through valleys, and over streams.

Before she could recognize her surroundings, she found herself inside a strange house. Fear struck with a vengeance. This place reeked of evil. She could feel it in her bones. Something awful was happening here. The lights were dim, some flickering mildly as Jenna drifted through a few rooms. Cracks ran across dingy walls. The planks of the floor were old and sagging, and a classic country tune played somewhere in the distance.

Ascending further through the house, the sound of someone grunting grew louder. She entered a wide-open living space and spotted a bald man dressed in army fatigues straddling a woman.

Oh my God, he was strangling her. Although Jenna

tried to shut her eyes, she found she had little control over her body. Horror settled over her as the woman clawed at the gloved hands of the person choking the life out of her. The whites of the girl's eyes turned blood red, then her lips went purple and cracked.

Veins bulged in the killer's neck and arms as he applied more pressure. The woman's heels slammed rhythmically against the floor. *Smack! Smack! Smack!*

The sound quivered through Jenna, and she wanted to wrestle the man away and scream until he stopped. In her paralyzed state, no such actions or words would come forward. All she could do was watch.

The woman went limp and Jenna's heart sank. Rage coiled through her at what she just witnessed. She was somebody's daughter, perhaps sister, and friend—and didn't deserve to die. The welling of tears rose in her chest at the senseless taking of human life.

After the killer released his victim and stood, Jenna was able to define every creak in the floor caused by the movements. He flexed his wrists and popped his neck as if completing a task that took a little more effort than expected. The mannerisms were familiar, as if she knew him from somewhere in the past.

It was the same man who murdered Sylvia Clark.

Snatching the girl by her hair, he dragged her body across the floor and propped her in a sitting position against the wall. He whistled along with the country ballad before disappearing into the kitchen. The ceiling fan spun round and round, casting fast-moving shadows across the wall, while the rickety light fixture bobbed back and forth.

And the dead girl stared straight ahead, seeing nothing.

The attacker hauled a large roll of Visqueen into the room. He spread it out on the floor and went for his victim.

Suddenly, he stopped and stood straight as an arrow. The sound of a female's voice ascending in a high-pitched melody filled the room. The killer somehow realized he wasn't the only one present in the room. And Jenna knew all the prayers in the world would not stop him from turning his head and taking notice of her.

Oh, God, please don't.

He gazed directly at her. The black eyes were as penetrating as a laser. Ice fire shot through her. Her heart pounded so hard she feared it would explode.

"Who are you?" He ran toward her, the metal dog tags hanging around his neck clinking loudly.

Jenna's reaction was to retreat as he advanced, but as before, her muscles wouldn't budge.

"Why are you here?" he screamed.

She stood there silent and trembling.

"What do you want with me?" he repeated. "Get out of my house. You don't belong here!"

After a shrill scream rang out, Jenna became aware she was no longer in the killer's house. Someone was grabbing her through the darkness, pulling on her arm. She fought adamantly, amazed that her ability to move had come back so quickly this time.

"Jenna, stop it! Calm down."

Who was this person, and why were they telling her to calm down?

"It's okay. Take it easy." The voice was familiar, and it registered the person wrestling her was Barbara. She stopped struggling and sat up.

"I heard you screaming from the living room. I think you're having a nightmare."

It was happening again. Her worst fear had come true. Except this time, the killer saw her.

Jenna turned on the lamp, then shielded her eyes from the brightness.

Barbara sank onto the mattress. "Are you okay?"

"Did you lock the front door before you went to bed? I don't remember doing it?"

Her friend peered around confused. "I…I don't know. It's like six o'clock in the morning. Why are you asking if the door is locked?"

"Can you go see if it is?"

Barbara threw out her hands. "Why?"

"Just do it, please. Hurry."

Shaking her head in disbelief, she strode out of the room.

"Are you checking?" Jenna called out.

"Yes, crazy person, I'm checking."

A minute later Barbara returned, hands on her hips. "The door is locked. What's this all about?"

"He's killed again."

"Who?"

"The one I told you about from my spirit walk. He strangled another girl tonight. There's one catch."

"What is that?

Jenna looked at her friend and without blinking, said, "This time he saw me."

"What?"

"He screamed at me and asked what I was doing there."

Barbara wandered to the chair across from the bed and sat. "Do you know how crazy this sounds?"

"You told me if this happened again then I'd have reason to worry. Remember that?"

Judging by the expression on her friend's face, Jenna could tell it hit home. "Okay, so I told you that. What are you going to do?"

"I'm going to have to go to the police."

Barbara chuckled. "They'll never believe you."

"I know."

"So why bother?"

"Because I'm witnessing women being murdered and can't sit back and do nothing. I have to at least try to report what I'm seeing and hope to God they take action."

"And do what?"

"I know what he looks like. And I saw the inside of his house."

"Do you think they'll take you seriously?"

"Won't know until I try."

"You're going to do this, huh?"

"I have to, Barbara. What am I supposed to do, wait until someone else dies?"

"Cole works at the precinct," her friend said.

Dammit. She'd forgotten.

"You just going to bounce in there after ten years of being MIA and tell him this?"

That just complicated things, didn't it? Perhaps, keeping this to herself would be the better option after all. She couldn't even imagine how to approach such a thing, and what his reaction to something like that would be. It was a bad idea all the way around.

The last time Jenna saw Cole was the dreadful day her parents found out the awful crimes his father had committed, and practically dragged her out of his house kicking and screaming. And add to that, there were the crazy heart palpitations every time thoughts about him emerged. What does someone say after all these years to the person they just up and walked out on in the middle of the hottest love affair they'd ever had, right after he was forced to deal with his father's atrocious sins? But innocent women were being killed, and she had a front-row seat to the murders as they were taking place. If she could help in any way…

"Guess I'm going with you," Barbara said.

She shook her head emphatically. "No way. How do you think he'll respond when he sees the two of us?"

"You don't have a snowball's chance in hell of getting through to him by yourself."

"How long has it been since you've talked to him?"

"Not long after you left, why?"

"It won't be much different than me going in there. He'll think you're just as crazy as I am."

"I've been a witness to your experiences."

She cocked her head, considering it. Then said, "I can't ask you to do that."

"You didn't. I offered."

Thank God Barbara came back at this exact time. Her best friend would come to the rescue again, like she had done so many times before. Leaving Texas without a word had been a selfish thing to do. Now seeing how truly upset those actions back then had made the greatest pal she'd ever had brought regret.

"I'm sorry, Barbara. I didn't tell you goodbye, and I was wrong for that. I have missed you so much, and I hope you can forgive me."

Her friend smiled. "I'm putting coffee on," she said, rising from the chair. "Go jump in the shower.

You're sweating like a pig. And as much as I'm not sure how you feel about Cole, you don't want him seeing you like this after ten years."

Yep, this was the Barbara she remembered, never the sentimental one, and pulling no punches, but the most loyal friend a girl could ever ask for. "Yeah, well, you're no princess yourself. Your hair looks like Medusa's."

Barbara grinned and strolled out of the room, hollering from the kitchen, "I clean up rather good in about five minutes. Now you, that'll take a lot more effort."

"Gee, thanks," Jenna yelled, getting out of bed, and heading toward the bathroom.

"Anytime." Barbara's voice floated through the shutting of the door.

****

Cole Rainwater stared at the autopsy report of Sylvia Clark. They had gotten no breaks in this case. Though more than seventy percent of the victim's body had been burned, the ME listed the cause of death as asphyxiation. The forensic review of the dead girl and the scene where she'd been discovered revealed no evidence linking the person who had killed her. Same with the results of the rape kit. No DNA, only traces of a lubricant. The bastard had used a condom.

Burning the body, using a condom, not leaving so much as a tire track or a footprint in the dirt: all methods to cover his tracks. There were two types of killers in this world. Those who killed on a whim, and those who meticulously planned their assaults. This guy was the latter. It made Cole sick to think they'd just began to see this perpetrator's handiwork.

He peered up from the autopsy report as Lucas Channing, a fellow homicide detective, rapped on his door. "Hey, buddy, there are two witnesses out here. They've got one helluva story. No one's sure what to make of it."

"Are you telling me this, or asking me to do something about it?" He already knew the answer. "Send them in."

"Thanks." Channing glanced back and motioned for the visitors to come into Cole's office.

He almost fell out of his chair as familiar faces peered into the room.

"Hello, Cole," Barbara Cassidy said as Jenna Langley stood there in his doorway.

He would have expected the devil himself before ever dreaming these two would have walked through his door.

But that was just what they did and sat in front of his desk as if they owned the place. Well, at least Barbara did. Pale-faced, Jenna looked like she'd rather be standing in front of a firing squad than staring at him across a desk.

The usual buzz of a precinct—the tapping of keyboards, phones ringing, people murmuring—faded into the distance as he stared at her. She wore her hair long now, straight and fashioned to the side. Gone were the loose curls that once crowned her forehead and the golden tendrils he once twined around his fingertips. She was all grown up and looking hot in that trim business suit.

He snapped back to reality. What the hell was this anyhow, some bizarre reunion after ten long years?

"I guess you want to know why we're here,"

Barbara said as if it was just another day.

"You her spokesperson, Barb?" he asked while glaring at Jenna. "Because from what I can remember, she's never had a problem speaking for herself."

"I don't need anybody to talk for me," Jenna snapped.

"Still the same smartass I see," Barbara remarked.

His eyes burned into her. "I was directing my question to her, not you." His attention traveled back to Jenna. "It sounded a lot like you were talking to me."

"It doesn't matter," Jenna broke in.

"How long have you been in Texas?" he asked, ignoring Barbara's annoyed sigh.

Jenna fidgeted uncomfortably in the chair, bouncing her attention around the room, finally settling on the brass nameplate adorning his desk. "I've been back for two weeks."

"Interesting. I haven't seen you. Hiding from me?" he sneered. "Again?"

"Does she look like she's hiding?" Barb squawked. "She's sitting right here in front of you."

Cole glared at the little wise-ass sitting next to Jenna, and said, "We have coffee in the bullpen. Why don't you go fix yourself a cup?"

As Barbara started to object, Jenna grabbed her arm and nodded. "It's okay."

"Are you sure?"

"Yeah, I'll be fine."

With that she stood and trudged to the door, but turned back. "If you need me, I'll be right out here."

"What is she, your bodyguard?" Cole remarked, watching Barbara clear the room.

"No," Jenna said quietly. "She's a good friend

trying to protect me."

For a moment he was distracted by someone strolling past his office door. Then her statement clicked. "Protect you. From me?"

He wanted to laugh. The way he remembered it, he had been the one who suffered a broken heart years ago. If anyone needed protection, it wasn't her.

So, she'd been back for two weeks, huh? He wondered how often any thoughts of him crossed her mind during that time.

Certainly not every day for the last ten years—which was how often thoughts like that crashed through his memory since the day she had walked out on him. Anger gave him courage this time around. "I take it your mission for coming here today isn't to see me."

"It's been ten years, Cole. What do you expect?"

Fire seeped into his veins. "That's right, and we were just dumb kids back then."

Jenna's chin slumped. "I didn't say that."

"You didn't have to. Your silence over the years has said it all."

Head snapping up, her eyes met his, fury gleaming in the glorious blue depths. "*My* silence? What about yours?"

He put up a hand to stave off any lie she might consider telling. Like he needed a tortured stroll down memory lane today from a woman who had cut him out of her life with the snap of a finger. God, she was more beautiful than he remembered. It was surreal, sitting across from the girl—now a woman—he saw damn near every night in his dreams.

"What are you here for, Jenna?"

He noticed how she clutched the purse in her lap

tightly, appearing as confident as a turkey on Thanksgiving Day. Good, uncomfortable. "What I'm about to tell you is going to sound nuts."

As crazy as you coming into my office after disappearing for ten years?

"I'm all ears.

She took a deep breath. "The girl who was murdered, Sylvia Clark."

"What about her?"

"I saw the murder." She said it as if she was spitting out a sour grape.

Cole leaned across his desk. "What?"

"But not in the way you might think. I saw it during an out-of-body experience."

"What are you talking about?"

Here came that body language again. The one telling him she'd rather be anywhere but here. In his office. In a police station. With him.

"I had a few of these experiences as a teenager. You remember, don't you?"

This must be a joke. "Did you hit your head or something?"

"I witnessed it, Cole. I wouldn't lie about that."

He narrowed his eyes, scrutinizing her. "Who said anything about a lie?"

She stood. "I know you think I'm lying, but I'm not. That isn't the only murder I've seen. Last night I had another spirit walk. Barbara was there when it happened."

Cole had no idea what possessed Jenna to come in here—after all these years—telling this wild story, but to see her in this state, he knew at once she believed it. He didn't know what concerned him more, the possibility Jenna was this crazy, or the reality she could be this conniving.

"Do you think I don't realize how insane this sounds?"

Or maybe on a much larger scale than you considered before coming in here.

"I'm having these experiences," she sputtered, moving behind her chair. "I've seen women being murdered, and I can't stand by and do nothing. That's why I had to come here today. I was hoping if I reported what I saw, you could help."

"You're telling me you witnessed a murder—and that it happened last night?"

"Yes." She sat back down. "I can describe the killer, and the house where the murder took place. I can even tell you what the victim looks like. She had blue eyes, light brown, curly hair, and wore a pair of small, turquoise earrings. I can go on if you want."

"What's her name?"

"I don't know."

"You said you saw the house the murder occurred in. Where is it?"

"I don't know that either. But I got a fairly good look at the inside."

"She's right," Barbara said, reappearing at the door, and leaning against it, coffee cup in hand. "I was at her house this morning right after the...*experience*."

"Great. your bodyguard is back," Cole muttered.

He couldn't imagine why Barbara encouraged this odd behavior, but he'd had about enough of it. "I don't know what made the both of you decide to come in here with this horseshit. This isn't some funny game; it's a serious case with a real, dead victim."

"You think we don't know this, Sherlock?" Barbara remarked.

"Evidently, you don't." Glaring at Barbara he imagined the joy of slapping the handcuffs on her and taking her into custody just for shits and giggles. But it would only put the poor guards through hell.

"Why don't you just hear her out, Cole? I believe she saw something."

For a brief second, he considered Barbara could be telling the truth. But this had to be the most outlandish tale he'd ever heard. Yeah, okay, Jenna told him about strange occurrences back when they were dating. He didn't put any stock in it then, and for damn sure wasn't going to change now. She should have outgrown such foolishness long ago.

He cleared his throat. "Thanks for coming in, but if you two will excuse me, I have a murder case to solve that isn't a figment of my imagination."

"You're a real asshole, Rainwater." Barbara stood and taking Jenna's arm, headed her toward the door.

"Yeah. *Real* being the key word here," he muttered. "I trust you can show yourselves out."

After they left, he shut the door and slumped in the chair, running his fingers through his hair. For the life of him, he'd probably never make sense of what just happened.

But one thing was clear, Jenna Langley still had the power to wreck his world.

****

At five p.m., the watch commander, Ronnie Beckett, ambled through Cole's office door, post-a-note in hand. "We gotta call at the front desk. A body's been found by the old railroad tracks."

Since the location Beckett mentioned was only a few miles from the precinct, Cole had a sinking premonition the corpse would be another victim of their guy. Although he feared he already knew the answer, he asked, "What condition is the body in?"

If he was wrong, he'd gladly breathe a huge sigh of relief.

"Set on fire."

"Damn."

The perp had no intention of letting up. Unfortunately, this was the way serial killers got caught. The more they killed, the better the chances they'd slip up. That wouldn't be any consolation to the loved ones of future victims, though. They needed to catch this bastard yesterday. Cole took the note, glanced at the address, and started around his desk.

Beckett warned him to grab a raincoat. "It's raining hard out there."

The fact he hadn't noticed the weather did not surprise him. Ever since *that* woman left his office this morning, causing a whirlwind of mixed emotions, and setting off a tidal wave of old memories, the whole day had been a blur. He grabbed a raincoat from the closet and headed out into the bullpen. It was time to go to work and get Jenna Langley off his mind.

He noticed right away Jeremy Gibbs, the other detective working the case, waited for him just outside the door. "Here we go again," Gibbs said, tossing him the keys to the cruiser. "Maybe he left some evidence this time."

They headed toward the exit. Cole hoped he was right. No detective ever wanted to give up on such a prospect. However, with this perpetrator, intuition told him things would not be so easy.

They arrived in record time. As Cole stepped out of the cruiser with Gibbs not far behind, he situated the hood of the raincoat over his head as a shield from the rain. The familiar van of the medical examiner's office was parked along the side of the road. He considered it strange that before these recent killings hit such a small community, he'd never even met the current ME. What had it been, two years since he came to work for the Farmersville PD?

In that time, he'd only handled a few homicide cases, and all of them had been small potatoes compared to this one. With the way things were heating up, the likelihood of being on a first-name basis with the pathologist by the end of the month was almost guaranteed. This reminded him of the good old days working for the Fort Worth PD.

Cole peered down the road, noticing at least ten news vans lining the street, then he carefully slogged over the slopes of the embankment to the other side of the railroad tracks. No doubt, this homicide would be splashed all over every major network within the hour. A sick feeling struck him. Memories came out of hiding, taking him back to the fallout of his father's actions ten years ago and the heavy price Cole paid.

The media had hounded him, camping outside the house, shoving microphones in his and his mother's face every time they stepped off the porch. And the most atrocious thing: the reality of the heinous crimes Derek Rainwater committed against those young women. When all was said and done, he scarcely had a friend left in high school. Parents didn't condone their children hanging out with the kid of a mass murderer.

The body lay on the wet ground, still smoldering. Cole wound his way through homicide detectives, and forensic technicians to get a better view. A strong odor of burning plastic, mixed with the scent of charred flesh, hung heavy in the air. The closer he got, the more apparent it became the victim was not burned as badly as the last one. Although the pouring rain may have put out the flames, it also could have washed away much-needed DNA.

After shouldering the rest of his way through the crowd, Cole gazed down at what was left of her face. Her blue eyes were open; the sclerae puddled with blood; lips were an angry purple and cracked. A sure sign of strangulation. Then he noticed the earring in her left ear. The stone inside the thin encasement was turquoise, just as Jenna told him.

He didn't believe in coincidences.

Neither did he buy into this whole out-of-body experience. Finding out what Jenna knew, and exactly how she knew it would be the next step. Enough with the bullshit.

Chapter Three

Agreeing to have dinner with Cole Rainwater was a huge mistake.

Even more tragic was the way the thought of it made her heart flutter. When he called this morning and invited her out tonight, no reason had been given for the invitation, but the headline in the morning paper revealed his motive. The girl she described to him had been found dead. He wanted information.

Strange, how just yesterday she'd been a nutcase he kicked out of his office.

As Jenna headed across the cantina to meet Cole, knots tightened in her stomach. After years of reliving the hellish day she'd been torn away from him, recalling the countless nights spent crying herself to sleep, Cole Rainwater was suddenly back in her life. But they weren't kids anymore.

And the carefree relationship they once had melted away with the passing years. Maturity and too much time apart had formed a wedge between them. And of course, there was the fact he never even tried to pursue her before she'd been forced to leave Texas. If you care about someone, you sure as hell don't just let them go so easily, do you? Having been away for quite a while, she had no idea who he was now. Although seeing him again at the police station brought back all the old, familiar emotions he'd always evoked in her.

As she peered across the diner, Cole waved from the table. Seeing his handsome face made her heart pound, palms become sweaty, and sent a tingling sensation rising in her cheeks. She needed to take a breath. No matter what, she couldn't let him see her this way. After all, this was just a casual meeting.

She approached the table and noticed right away that he wasn't dressed in a business suit like he had been earlier today. He appeared comfortable in a pair of jeans and a navy blue collar shirt. He stood, pulling out her chair. Yet the expression on his face was far from charming. "Thanks for coming," he said dryly, retaking his seat.

Judging by the amount of heat creeping up her face, her cheeks must be as red as a fire hydrant. She ignored the unsettling effect and sat down. "I didn't have anything planned, so…"

"I ordered us a margarita."

"I see that." She might need about eight more to get through this. But not if it meant being at his mercy to get her home. She'd rather walk to the rental house naked in seven-degree weather.

"Strictly for the sake of curiosity, what brings you to Texas again?"

She sipped the drink, working extra hard to keep her trembling hand under control. "Business. I have a client here."

"And what kind of business is that?" he asked, showing no interest in her answer.

She gave a nonchalant expression. Two can play this game, she decided. "I'm a consultant for the janitorial industry."

He frowned, and she caught a glimpse of intrigue.

"That's unusual. How did you get into that?"

"I owned a similar company and sold it a few years ago. I found that consulting is much easier than dealing with employees who don't like to show up for work."

"I can see your point."

"I never saw you as the detective type."

He averted his attention and cleared his throat.

His reaction told her this was a delicate subject. She averted her gaze. "It's none of my business."

"No, it's fine. Working for the homicide unit is not something I would have ever thought I'd end up doing. But after what happened with my father, I think I felt it was my sole responsibility to stop all the monsters in the world. I wasn't successful at stopping him."

"It was never your job to stop him, Cole. You didn't know what he was doing. None of us did."

He laughed, but it wasn't a pleasant gesture. "You didn't stick around to be my therapist back then. What makes you think I need your help now?"

A woman's loud chatter swept passed her, and she turned as a server escorted a young couple to their table only a few feet from them. As she considered his cruel words, it struck her as ironic that he didn't seem to care if she stuck around at all. He had plenty of time to let her know his feelings. But he never even tried, and just let her go.

She opened her mouth to respond, and he said, "I realize the son of a mass murderer isn't the ideal boyfriend."

Another low blow. "Did you think what your father did had any bearing on the way I felt about you?"

"Your parents split us up because of it. You were all too willing to go along with them."

So, this was what he really thought. And what about his part in all of it, or better yet, lack of? Did he expect her to go running after someone who did not want her anymore? "How dare you try to turn this into my fault."

The server appeared, ready to take their order, disrupting their conversation.

She'd completely lost her appetite. Yet after listening to Cole ramble off what he wanted, it became apparent his hunger had not been affected in the least.

To hell with him. If he could order something, so could she. Jenna chose chips and queso, and of course another margarita. If things kept going this way, the first alcoholic beverage would be gone within the next minute or two.

The waitress walked off and the woman at the nearby table dropped a fork. It clanged loudly against the ceramic tile, unnerving Jenna.

Cole cleared his throat again, saying, "I'm sorry. I shouldn't have acted that way. Just like you said at the precinct. It's been ten years. We have both grown up and moved on."

Jenna found it amazing how easily he packed their love affair away as if the memories had never been created. All those nights of lying awake crying, wondering how she would survive without him had just been cheapened by his indifferent attitude. Well, at least it was good to know that they'd moved on though. At any rate, he had.

"The reason I invited you here tonight—I have some questions about the murder you saw."

Of course, he did. However, gone was the intention to make it so painless for him. "I'm confused," she said with sarcasm. “Why would you want to question me about that? When I tried to tell you what I saw, you threw me out of your office, remember?”

“Out of body experiences, Jenna. C’mon.”

“I know how it sounds, okay? We haven’t seen each other in how long? Do you really think I wanted to come into the police station and tell you that if it wasn’t true?”

He didn’t seem interested in her reasoning. “You said you saw the killer. Tell me about him.”

“Fine.” She sighed, attempting to reign in her anger. “He’s bald. I’d place his age around sixty. Tall, solid guy. He has a goatee and gray eyes. Wears army fatigues and dog tags.”

He narrowed his attention on her and sat there silently.

“What?”

“You just described my father, Jenna.”

Jesus, she never considered that aspect. But now that he mentioned it…was that why the guy seemed so familiar? No, it couldn’t be. Derek Rainwater committed suicide ten years ago. Glaring at Cole, she had no clue what to say.

“Is this some kind of sick joke?” he demanded.

“Now wait a minute. I didn’t say he looked like your father. You did.”

“Because that’s exactly who you described.”

“I told you what and who I saw.”

The way he stared at her made her suspicious there was something wrong with her. Then he said, “I’m going to be honest. I don’t believe in this spirit walk crap. But I think you saw something. I don’t know how, but the victim we found last night is the same one you told me about at the precinct. I want to know how that's possible, Jenna."

She stared at him nonplussed. "I told you. This is what I saw during an out-of-body experience, just like the last victim, Sylvia Clark."

His penetrating gray eyes held her gaze with the force of an industrial-strength magnet. "Then why didn't you come forward after she died?"

"Because at first, I didn't realize it was real. And when I discovered it was, well, for the same reason you don't believe me now."

"Dammit, Jenna." Frustration and anger flashed in his eyes. "People are dying, and I need you to shoot straight with me right here and now."

"I am, damn you."

"The hell you are."

Loud whooping laughter erupted from the right side of the diner where patrons watched an NBA game on the big screen over the bar. After blocking out the noise, she deeply regretted reporting her experiences to Cole. Although she realized it was a big pill to swallow, she didn't expect such treatment. So much for trying to do the right thing. He had no intention of taking this seriously. She stood, fished through her purse, and threw a twenty-dollar bill on the table.

"Where are you going?"

"Home."

"We haven't eaten yet."

"I'm not hungry."

He stood. "Jenna, sit down. Don't be ridiculous."

She glared at his face, feeling every ounce of anger focusing directly on him. It wasn't just his distrustful attitude, although that alone would certainly be enough.

It was how he'd abandoned her years ago, and then casually mentioned they'd simply grown up and moved on. How convenient.

"I'm leaving, and you can go to hell."

****

By the time Jenna made it back to the rental house, her blood had reached the boiling point. She'd hashed over Cole's cruel treatment the entire trip. Working to unlock the door, her hand trembled with anger. Once the deadbolt disengaged, she swung the door open, trounced inside, and slammed it. That son of a bitch.

She headed toward the light switch in the living room. Perhaps he had been asleep for the whole month after they had broken up because his memories surrounding those details from ten years ago were disillusioned as hell. He'd twisted things around and had the gall to place the blame for everything at her feet. Yet he damn well knew she had no control over what happened. Neither one of them would ever escape the horrible day when news of what Cole's father had done was broadcast all over every channel in the metroplex.

Derek Rainwater committed suicide by dousing himself with gasoline and setting his body on fire inside the work van where the burned corpses of two missing teens were also discovered. A few days before that, Jenna recalled the police coming around Cole's house asking questions about a missing girl from a few towns over. A witness had placed Derek's van in the vicinity of the kidnapping. The authorities speculated that he had killed himself because he knew they were closing in, and he had no way out.

After it all began to unravel, and everyone learned

the grisly details of the crimes Cole's father had committed, Jenna recalled with a heavy heart how Amanda Langley wrecked the relationship she had with her boyfriend. Her parents monitored her every move back then. There was no getting out of the house for fear she'd go running to him.

And she would have, given the opportunity.

After making her way to the bathroom, the woman in the mirror stared back at her, watching each earring come off. The reflection was nothing more than the grown-up face of a teenage girl who'd fallen head over heels in love with Cole Rainwater.

She recalled his words from earlier tonight. Perhaps he had moved on, but that hadn't been in the cards for her.

After washing up and dressing for bed, she wandered into the bedroom and flipped on the television. No use lying down now. The aftereffects of meeting with Cole tonight made sleeping an impossibility.

The moment the TV came on, she was gripped by a powerful vision. Her body sank into the armchair, hand clutching the armrest for dear life.

An ear-piercing scream sliced through the night, and Jenna witnessed a girl with strawberry blonde hair standing in the darkness, paralyzed by fear as a man charged straight for her.

About the time the young woman snapped out of immovability and took off running, the shadowy figure with the black hoodie grabbed his hostage quick as lightning. He put a hand over her mouth, leaned into her ear, and whispered, "Scream again, and I'll snap your fucking neck."

He moved his hand away to get a stronger hold on her. The victim whimpered and begged. “Please, don’t kill me.”

He placed a knife against her throat and said, “Start moving,” while thrusting her in the direction of the isolated area between two houses from which he’d emerged just moments ago.

Oh God, no, not again.

Jenna knew upon arriving home, she had been fully awake and hadn’t gone to sleep. How was this happening?

The girl began sobbing now, as the killer forced her through the narrow easement, past a chain length fence, and out into the front lawn of a house.

A dog barked and the kidnapper ushered her away from the open area, against some shrubs. Applying more pressure to the knife, he again threatened to make good on his promise if she dared to make a sound.

A sliding glass door opened, and a porch light came on. Someone stepped from the house, ordering the dog to be quiet.

Jenna tried to scream at the man standing in the light. No sound emerged. It was the same as the last time. She had no voice.

The guy wandered over to his barking dog, and peered over the fence, as the dog jumped against it, growling.

With every second that ticked by, Jenna silently pled with the man to turn his head to the left, spot the dark figures pressed against the bushes. They were right there.

Horror settled over her as the fellow shook his head, soothed the dog, and unsnapped the chain from the animal's leash. "C'mon, Harley," he said, leading him into the house, and sliding the door shut. The porch light went out, dashing any hope Jenna held out for the girl's rescue.

Yet as the killer once again forced her along the tree line, an uneven patch of the ground caused him to lose his footing. He fell, taking the victim down, too.

The petrified young woman clawed out from under him, somehow avoiding his attempt at recapture, and stumbled to her feet. With no time to lose, she dashed across the grass, screaming bloody murder.

Jenna observed the scene with bated breath as the perpetrator stumbled quickly to his feet and took off after the girl.

The porch light snapped back on, and the sliding glass door slid open. The dog bounded from the house, with its owner running across the yard not far behind. "Are you okay?" the man yelled, as the scared young woman ran toward his fence.

"Help me!" she cried, attention fixed on the darkness over her shoulder.

"My God, what happened?" Holding the dog by the collar, the guy unlatched the gate and swung it open to allow her passage.

The victim pointed a trembling finger into the black of night, beyond the fence. "That…that man…he…he tried to kidnap me."

But no one was there.

Jenna snapped back to the present with a sharp inhale. Sweat poured down her face, blurring her vision. The noise of the television made it evident she was back in the rental. With a hand over her chest, she concentrated on calming her pounding heart, taking deep, easy breaths.

Legs trembling, she used the support of the armrest to steady herself and stood. What the hell just happened? That was no out-of-body experience, or was it? The last few times the phenomenon had occurred, she'd been sleeping, but not this time. This new development unsettled her to her core. How could this be taking place while she was wide awake? The best thing to do would be to sit for a minute, think. But her head hurt.

She searched for some aspirin and popped two pills in her mouth, chasing them down with bottled water. What was she going to do now?

****

Legs stretched out, and boots crossed, resting on a footstool. Cole lounged in a chair on his front porch, He took the last swig of beer and set the empty bottle on the table. Ever since Jenna left the restaurant, thinking about her had been a nonstop activity. He laughed to himself. Who was he kidding? From the moment that woman waltzed into the precinct, his mind hadn't strayed from her.

Tonight, seeing her standing there by the candlelight in that sexy dress, with the long, honey-colored hair cascading down her shoulders, it had been nearly impossible to keep from gathering her into his arms and kissing the spitfire right out of her. God knows the burning desire to do much more than that had been going on for years.

But their past wasn't that simple, was it? His father's crimes came between them years ago. And her parents keeping them away from each other once they found out the truth seemed to be the final nail in the coffin of what they once had. Why couldn't she have at least faced him though, answered the door when he showed up at her house, came to the phone when he called, or responded to his dozens of letters?

He needed to stop it. It was over. The time for moving on once and for all had come. After all, she had left his memories in the dust, hadn't she?

His cell phone rang, and he snatched it off the table. Her number popped up. After getting the heatwave under control, he cleared his throat before answering. "Hello?"

"Cole, I'm sorry to disturb you this late."

According to his watch, it was just about midnight. "I was awake anyhow. Is everything all right?"

"I think so."

"What's wrong?"

"I had another episode."

"Back to that again."

She sighed and then, "Look, I know you don't believe me, but I thought you should hear this."

He got up, sauntered into the kitchen, and grabbed another beer out of the fridge. He had a suspicion it would be needed before this was through. He waited until popping the top, and said, "Okay, shoot."

"I saw a girl being kidnapped. She has strawberry blonde hair. Lots of freckles. She had on a gray, zip-up sweater, blue jeans, and a pair of purple, glittery shoes. I'm quite sure the guy who tried to kidnap her is the same one I've been seeing."

"Wait…tried to kidnap her?"

At least twenty seconds ticked by before Jenna answered. "She escaped."

A few beers might not do the trick. It might come

down to a fifth of Jack Daniels. “So, you’re calling to tell me about a kidnap victim who was never abducted? That sound about right?”

“Do you think this is a joke?”

“If it is, it’s not very amusing, Jenna.”

“I’m just trying to help you, ya know.”

“I’m not the one who needs help. Perhaps you should consider calling a psychiatrist.”

“Now wait a minute—”

“No, you wait a minute. I don’t know what you’re thinking, or how you imagine this little charade of yours will pan out, but it’s pissing me off. You haven’t offered anything of real value to this case, have you?”

“That’s not true.” She had the nerve to sound offended. “I gave you information on the last victim, didn’t I?”

“Who is dead,” he reminded her. “Your so-called episodes did not save the girl. And in case you haven’t noticed, the bastard who killed her is still at large. We have no leads. So, tell me, how have you helped?”

“I’m trying.”

“To do what, exactly? That’s what I can’t figure out. Why won’t you just level with me?”

“What do you want me to tell you?”

“You can start with the truth. How did you have a description of the victim before we found the body?

“I told you. I saw her.”

“Bullshit, Jenna.”

Another call beeped in. Cole snatched the phone away and glanced at the contact. It was Gibbs, his partner at the precinct. Odd he’d be calling this time of night. “Listen, “I’ve got an important call coming in. I’ve got to go.”

When she didn't respond, he clicked over. "Hey, man. What's up?"

"Um, a girl and her neighbor just came into the station about five minutes ago. The young woman is saying she was attacked and managed to run to safety at the neighbor's house. It sounds like this might be the work of our guy."

Cole grabbed his keys and headed toward the door. "Keep them there. I'm on my way."

"You got it, partner."

He strode to his car, hoping this new development had nothing to do with the almost-kidnapped girl Jenna called him about. And if it did, a clear answer as to how she knew about that would be in order. He'd damn well get the truth out of her this time.

****

Cole swung into the precinct and rushed through the doors. It was past midnight, and there were only a handful of officers and staff working the night shift.

The dispatcher pointed toward Gibbs' office.

He caught her drift and headed in that direction.

Cole rapped on Gibbs' door before opening it. His partner glanced his way, motioning for him to come inside.

"This is Detective Rainwater," Gibbs said to the two people sitting in front of his desk, as they glanced over at him.

The farther Cole advanced into the room, the better he could see them. The male appeared to be around the age of fifty-five, with salt and pepper hair, an unshaven face, and warm eyes. The female was young, perhaps sixteen or seventeen years old, slender face, and porcelain skin dotted generously with freckles. Her hair, strawberry blonde. His attention immediately roamed to her feet. Her legs were crossed, one foot swinging out in front of the other. She wore a pair of Converse shoes. The color…a glittery purple.

It didn't surprise him. He had a hunch before leaving his house, the victim would match Jenna's description. He cleared his throat, directing his attention to the girl. "Hi. Detective Gibbs tells me you had quite the scare tonight."

The girl nodded as Cole grabbed another chair and hauled it around to the other side of her, positioning it so she faced him. He sat down and leaned in closer. "Can you tell me what happened?"

Her gaze shifted from him, to Gibbs, and back to Cole again. He smiled attempting to ease the witness. "It's okay. I know you already told Detective Gibbs your story. And I realize this is upsetting for you, but we've discovered sometimes when a person tells a story a second time, they remember certain details they didn't recall the first time around."

She appeared deep in thought and then frowned as if accepting his reasoning.

"Why don't you start from the beginning?"

"Well, I was visiting my friend, Jason. He picked me up earlier in the night like he usually does when he gets out of theatre class. We always drive back to his house to hang out for a few hours. And then I walk home from his place, which is only a few blocks from mine."

"You're in high school, right?"

"Yes. I attend Farmersville High."

"So you live at home with your parents?"

"Yes. They're right outside. They drove me here."

Cole reflected back to when he entered the precinct. Her mom and dad must have been the older couple sitting on the bench right inside the front doors.

"And this gentleman with you, it was his house you ran to after the attack, is that right?"

She nodded, and the guy in question extended his hand, saying, "My name is Elijah Williams."

Cole shook the man's hand and then returned his attention to the girl. "So you were at your friend's house."

"Yes. I left there at about, oh, I think eleven o'clock. I don't know if this creep was waiting for me or what, but as soon as I passed Jason's place, he ran between two houses and grabbed me."

"Did he have a weapon?"

She nodded emphatically. "He had a knife, and at one point, as he forced me along in front of Elijah's house and his dog started barking, he pulled me against the bushes and threatened to cut me if I made a sound. That was when he," she said, gesturing toward the neighbor, "came outside and turned on his porch light because the dog was making so much noise."

Cole examined the guy sitting next to her and said, "Did you see what happened?"

Elijah shook his head. "I didn't see anything when I went out and investigated the first time. I gathered the dog and brought him into the house because I figured there must have been a squirrel running up the tree, getting Harley excited. I was afraid he'd keep the neighbors awake half the night with his barking."

"It wasn't until the guy tripped and I broke free," the girl continued, "that I started screaming and running toward Elijah's house. He heard me and ran outside with his dog. I think that's what scared the man off."

"That's exactly what happened." the neighbor said. "I brought her into the house, and she called her parents. We all decided it would be best to go to the police and report what happened. But I didn't see the guy who was after her."

Cole asked, "Did you get a good look at your attacker?"

"It was so dark, and he was wearing a black hoodie. I never saw his face." Her expression became pensive, and she added as an afterthought, "Wait a minute. Could the guy have been the same jerk who offered me a ride while I was waiting for Jason to pick me up?"

Cole's attention traveled to Gibbs, who shrugged his shoulders, indicating it was the first he'd heard of this. "Someone tried to give you a ride before the attack?"

"Yes," she said, the expression in her eyes growing more convinced the stranger who offered a ride earlier in the night could very well have been the attacker. "He pulled up while I was sitting on the curb across from the gas station waiting for my friend and asked if I wanted him to drive me home. I said no, but he wouldn't go away. I just figured he was some creep trying to hit on me. And when Jason pulled up, he finally drove off."

"So you saw his vehicle?" Cole asked.

"It was brown and small. Looked like something from the seventies." She shook her head, disappointed. "I'm just not all that great with cars. I can't tell you what kind it was." Then an idea lit her eyes. "But ya know, my friend Jason collects models. He's great with things like that. And he did see the guy when he pulled in behind him."

"Do you think your friend Jason is still awake?"

"Nope. He was half asleep on the couch when I left his house."

"What about a description of the man who offered you a ride. Did you get a decent look at him?"

"Sorry. The hood was pulled up over his head and he had on sunglasses."

Cole stood and said, "Why don't you give Jason's phone number to Detective Gibbs? We'll give him a call in the morning." He fished a card out of his wallet and handed it to the young woman. "Here's my number. Call me if you remember anything else. We will keep you posted on the investigation. Thanks so much for coming in."

As he walked out of the room, he decided Jenna Langley had some more explaining to do.

Chapter Four

Cole slipped past a shocked Jenna without waiting for an invitation to enter. "The lights were on. I figured you were awake."

"I imagine you found out where I'm staying the same way you got my number."

"I'm a detective."

She shut the door and put her hand out to the couch. "Since you're here, have a seat."

"I'd rather stand."

Cole peered around. The rental Jenna was staying in was attractive at first glance, but there were small signs the landlord wasn't keeping up with repairs, such as an obvious water stain in the corner of the ceiling, and a few thin cracks running down the walls, which was an obvious sign of a leveling problem. At least the rental car outside was a beauty. It must have been one of the best rides on the lot. That, coupled with the expensive suit she'd worn into his office today told him she'd made a decent living.

"Suit yourself," she said, sitting down.

"Where were you tonight?"

"With you, remember?"

"That was until after nine. I'm talking about after."

"I came back here. Where do you think I went?"

"You called at midnight to tell me about a girl who almost got kidnapped. I didn't even get off the phone with you when my partner called to tell me there is some young lady in his office saying a guy tried to abduct her. And that's not even the bizarre part."

As he closed in, she shrank farther into the cushion. "Do you want to know the strange thing? The young woman matches the description you gave me on the phone, down to the purple glitter shoes, just like the dead girl we pulled out of the bushes yesterday with the turquoise earrings."

She stood. Her face couldn't have been more than ten inches from his. Her eyes were as wide as saucers. "You think I had something to do with this?"

If Cole didn't know better, he'd swear the flabbergasted expression on her face was genuine. "There are only two ways you'd know that information, Jenna. Either you were there when it happened, or you know the killer who did it."

"I have been trying to tell you, I—"

Disgusted, he backed away. "Don't bother. I don't want to hear anymore."

She rounded on him. "The rental I've been driving has a GPS tracker. If you think I was involved in this, you're welcome to check the device. You'll find the car has been parked in that same spot," she said, pointing outside the window, "since I got home from the restaurant."

As frustrated as Jenna might have made him in the past, he'd never wanted to throttle her as much as he did now. But she had gotten too close a moment ago; the sweet smell of her perfume was intoxicating. If he was honest, he'd admit the thought of drawing her into his arms and pouring the last bit of resistance he had into a heated kiss was overwhelming. He shouldn't be the same fool he had been ten years ago. "Where's your bathroom?" he said, unable to control the hoarse sound in his voice.

"The one in the hallway doesn't work. The landlord is coming tomorrow to fix it. You'll have to go to the end of the hall and use the one in the master bedroom."

After finishing in the bathroom, he opened the door leading into the bedroom. The object sitting on the bedside table caused his heart to skip a beat. He stepped over to the picture frame and took it into his hands. Gazing at their young faces stirred something deep within him.

It was a professional photo and had been taken when they were sixteen years old. Jenna had talked him into going to the studio to have it done. It had been so important to her, that deciding against his better judgment to make her happy turned out to be the greatest reward at the time. He always hated himself in photos. But staring at it now brought about a different reaction. He couldn't believe she kept this photograph after all these years. And it was as equally surprising to find it sitting on the table next to her bed.

He headed down the hall carrying the picture with him when the sound of Jenna's phone ringing caused him to stop. Secretly listening in on her conversation was intrusive, but he couldn't resist.

"Why are you up so late?" she said, then, "I know, I miss you too, honey. But I'll be home soon, and I can't wait to see you." A minute ticked by and she laughed. "That'll be fun. We'll do that when I get back. Why don't you get some sleep? You have a busy day tomorrow, and I'll call you first thing in the morning. I love you too, sweetheart."

Anger surged through Cole as he listened while she talked to her lover back home. There was picture of him next to her bed, yet she had a boyfriend, or husband, for all he knew, waiting in Georgia. What a phony she turned out to be.

He strode into the room as she put the phone on the table. It was impossible to ignore her surprise when she glanced up to see him standing there. Jenna cleared her throat. He placed the frame on the coffee table, turned the picture in her direction, and said tightly, "I wonder, does your significant other know you keep a picture of me on your nightstand."

"You mean my daughter?"

"That was your daughter?

"Yes."

"You have a daughter?"

"Yes."

He didn't know what disturbed him more, the fact she might have had a lover or the reality a kid was involved…another man's kid. The history she had with someone else shouldn't be his concern, should it? What an ass for having reacted with such jealousy at the thought she might be interested in someone other than him. It wouldn't have been out of the ordinary. The affair between them ended a long time ago.

"Does it surprise you that I kept this picture?"

She was breaking his resolve quickly. He needed to get a grip. And yet…

"Why didn't you answer any of my phone calls, Jenna? You didn't respond to my letters, and I must have sent a dozen of them." Crossing this line with her would surely cause more heartache. But it couldn't be helped. He had to know why she ignored him.

"What are you talking about? You never called. I didn't get any letters from you."

Searching her expression, it was obvious she was dumbfounded. "I came by your house several times. Your mother told me you didn't want to talk to me."

"That's not true." Then, as realization settled on her face, she slumped onto the couch. "Oh my God."

He joined her, and they both sat in silence.

"I can't believe my mom hid that from me."

"She never liked me," Cole remarked.

"If it's any consolation, that woman despised all of my friends."

He studied her face. Staring dead at her, he said, "I wish I would have known. I thought you didn't want anything to do with me."

"That's not how I felt about you. After everything that happened with your dad, I just assumed it was too much for you to deal with. So when my parents forbid me to see you, I thought you gave up on us."

"Funny. I thought you felt that way about me because of my father."

"No. I loved you. None of that mattered."

Loved? As in past tense.

That had been the story of their relationship. The affair happened long ago, and it had come to an end two years later. They had been away from each other too long. So much had taken place in between that time. How could he expect her to still love him? She'd moved on, even had a daughter with someone else. It was over, and the time came to finally accept that.

"It's late," he said, standing and heading toward the door. "We both need some sleep." Staring back at her, the words “Goodnight, Jenna” tumbled from his mouth. Then he slipped out.

****

The killer couldn’t believe the bitch got away. More than fifteen years had passed since someone escaped him. He had gotten to be a real pro at committing these crimes. But one slip-up had the potential to bring his freedom to an end. Last night served as a perfect example. He was still beating himself up over it. That level of recklessness should have never happened. Yet, if it hadn’t been for the nosey neighbor, recapturing the little tramp would have been easy.

Being on the prowl again so soon after last night’s debacle wasn’t smart. The killer knew better than anyone he should wait. At least taking a break would allow him to sit back and see if any damage came from his actions. But it had been dark during the pursuit. He was certain she didn’t see his face. Besides, the desire to feed this ravenous need burned deep in his gut. Seeing the latest victim escape only heightened the feeling.

He needed relief. If not, the hunger would become so consuming it would cause him to make additional sloppy mistakes. He couldn’t afford for that to happen. Taking precautions this time and traveling more than two hours away from his usual hunting grounds to find a victim would lessen the chance of getting caught.

And this girl had all the makings of the perfect prey. He’d been stalking her for several hours now, making sure to stay out of the view of any cameras. She was a smoker and using binoculars earlier in the day, he’d watched her step outside the convenience store where she worked to take a cigarette break. The interludes were every thirty to forty minutes. It was such a small town the store didn't get much traffic. He chose this place for that exact reason.

The sun was going down and figuring her shift would soon be coming to an end, he'd wait. From all appearances, she'd be well worth the time invested. The moment the girl had caught his eye, standing there in front of the store as he passed by, her attention drawn to the cell phone, he wanted her. She was preferably young and couldn't weigh more than one hundred and ten pounds. Smaller women made the best targets because they lacked the strength to fight back. Picturing a fistful of her long, black hair wrapped around his hand while he ravaged and tortured her made for a delightful image. She'd be his to explore the most unthinkable desires with. And the best part about it was the little whore had no idea what he planned to do to her. Living out a fantasy with her was a heart-racing thought. She'd be one delicious bitch. And he could feel the arousal of anticipation.

A car swung into the empty parking lot of the store, and a chubby guy got out with the same color shirt as the cashier he'd been watching. The girl's shift was finally over, and this fellow would be her replacement. His breathing increased. Excitement shot through him. The hunt had begun.

He started his car and waited for her to come out of the store. Fifteen minutes went by, and she strolled out, purse over her shoulder and car keys in hand. She headed for a small, compact car parked around the side of the building and climbed in.

She backed out of the parking space, and he

followed far enough behind as not to spook the target. As she turned onto a white rock road, he stayed out of view while tailing her. Then the brake lights came on and the car slowed. The girl was preparing to veer into her driveway. Ahead, her car made a direct maneuver after passing a mailbox. He would have to time the abduction perfectly before she made it to the house.

He pulled off to the side of the road and quickly got out, turning back at the last minute, almost forgetting the chloroform and cloth. Couldn't take the risk of another screaming target getting away. After dousing the material with the narcotic, he made fast tracks down the road.

His breathing was labored reaching the end of her driveway, and he feared she had already gone into the house. But when he turned the corner she reappeared, standing next to the open car door, talking on the phone. Thank God the call most likely delayed her. There were no other vehicles parked in front of the house. Approaching, luck was on his side. She leaned into the car to get her purse. With the perfect moment arising, he closed in, covering her face with the chloroform-soaked cloth. She only struggled a few seconds before going limp.

"C'mon, sugar," he said, tossing the unconscious body over his shoulder, and heading down the driveway. "I've got big plans for you."

****

Cole sat at his desk, mulling over all the leads, or lack of they had managed to gather in this case so far. It was a disheartening assessment to say the least. Canvassing the neighborhood where the young girl from the night before had almost been kidnapped, produced no results. They conducted a door-to-door sweep, but nobody saw anything out of the ordinary. The one promising lead they had, the girl's friend, Jason Cheng, who had possibly seen the suspect's car, was out of town for the day attending a funeral and wouldn't return until later in the evening. The department already left several messages for him to call them back as soon as possible.

As for the dead victim found in the bushes on the other side of the railroad tracks, after processing the scene, they found no fingerprints, hair follicles, or clothing fibers left behind by the killer. And just like Sylvia Clark, they could tell she had not been killed in the spot where her body had been recovered. They'd have to wait this time for the results of the rape kit.

Cole glanced at his watch. It was a little after eight p.m. With each passing day, they found nothing new to go on. They needed clues to track this monster down. Even though he realized leads could take a little time, and sometimes all it took was one to crack a case, the more time that slipped by, the less chance they'd have to bring this killer to justice. They needed to strike while the iron was hot.

This feeling of helplessness sucked, and knowing this case was not the only thing responsible for it made things even worse. Jenna Langley played a huge role. All the nights spent imagining what seeing her again would be like did nothing to prepare for the reality of it. What he'd say and how she'd react. She stepped out of his life so unexpectedly. Back then there hadn't been a worry of being without her. Today, he was afraid Jenna would disappear again, causing him to suffer once more. He shouldn't let that woman get too close this time. And it was foolish to believe that hadn't already happened.

The unexpected discovery last night complicated things. She had not tried to avoid him before leaving Texas. Her mother purposely hid his visits to keep them apart. That should not have made a difference. Ten years had gone by. But the truth was it made all the difference in the world.

So what was Jenna trying to pull now? Admittedly, there were things in the psychic world he didn't understand, and even with acknowledging a few episodes she'd had when they were teens, these claims of spirit walking and visions now had to be far-fetched as hell. It appeared all too convenient she was doing this involving a case he hadn't had the greatest luck in solving. Perhaps she'd been trying to get revenge because she thought he didn't care about her? The idea of that rang bogus. He knew her, dammit. That kind of conniving behavior wasn't like her. Then what was it?

The office phone rang, causing him to jump. He picked it up. "Detective Rainwater."

"Jason Cheng. You asked that I call you back."

"Yes. We are investigating the attack on your friend, Jessica, from last night. We had some questions for you. Can you come by now?"

"Uh, sure. Can you give me about fifteen minutes?"

"Yeah. I'll be here. See you then."

About damn time. Now they'd get somewhere.

****

When Jenna opened the door to let Barbara in, she didn't expect a slender, dark-haired woman to be standing next to her. Her friend had called ahead to say she was coming but hadn't mentioned bringing someone with her.

Before Jenna could get one word out, Barbara said, "This is Professor Delaney. She studies psychic phenomena at the Paranormal Research Center."

Jenna stood there, mouth open.

Barbara stared at her for a moment, as if Jenna ought to know bringing a stranger to someone's house unannounced was a perfectly normal thing to do. "She knows all about your out-of-body experiences."

"Wonderful," Jenna said through clenched teeth. She reprimanded her friend with a scowl while stepping aside for them to enter.

"It's so nice to meet you, Jenna," Delaney said, while Jenna closed the door.

"You, too," she lied behind a fake smile. Barbara had officially lost her mind and would damn well get an earful after this.

"I hope it's okay, but Barbara here told me all about what has been happening to you. I know a lot about this sort of thing, and I thought I could help."

"So you know Barbara?" Jenna asked.

"No. We just met tonight."

Of course you did.

This wasn't the first time Barbara showed up at her front door with people neither one of them knew…on a whim. Barbara should have outgrown this impetuous behavior by now. But the longer she stayed in Texas, the more obvious it became some things never changed.

"I've been doing lots of research today," her friend said, appearing quite proud. "I ran across the professor's website. I gave her a call and explained the situation. And here she is."

All in a day's work, huh?

"Imagine that." It took a minute for Jenna to gather her wits. "Where are my manners?" She eyed the professor and her friend who did not yet know how dead she was, and said, "Please have a seat."

As soon as the professor settled in on the couch, she said, "I have been conducting research and doing studies on psychic phenomena for the better part of twenty years now. And I have to tell you none of my subjects have had near the experiences Barbara tells me you've had."

"I'd like to be clear, professor," Jenna remarked, "I have no interest in letting someone study what has been happening to me."

"No, dear, that's not my intention. I understand you're having a difficult time coming to terms with the things that are occurring. This is where I was hoping to help."

"What do you mean?"

"Many people who have true clairvoyant abilities are confused, and even frightened by the phenomenon. I want to let you know you're not alone. And more importantly, you're not crazy. This kind of thing happens to millions of people all over the world. But like you, they don't understand it, and they fear people will label them as insane if they come forward."

Jenna took a deep breath, amazed at how comforting it was to hear a professional say that. Until now, Barbara had been her only outlet. Cole thought she was a nutcase. "You said you haven't met anyone that has had the experiences I've been having."

"Well, not as vivid as yours. What is happening to you is called remote viewing. It is the practice of seeking impressions about a distant or unseen object. You can see things that are hidden from physical view. This form of phenomena can be done through visions, or out of body travel."

"Oh my God. So that's why."

The professor stared at her, waiting for an explanation.

"Until the other night, all of these occurrences were taking place while I was asleep. But I had one when I was wide awake, and I couldn't understand it."

"Exactly. What's happening to you is not uncommon. Can I ask you something?"

Jenna nodded.

"Do you often see people surrounded by musical notes or certain colors?"

Shocked that the women would know that, Jenna admitted, "Colors."

The professor smiled. "The term for that is synesthesia. Your senses are heightened. You are more in tune with your surroundings than most people. How often do you experience déjà vu?"

"All the time."

"Jenna, I'd say you have otherworldly talents, or what some like to refer to as psychic abilities."

"But what if I don't want them? How can I turn them off?"

She chuckled. "I'm not surprised to hear you say that. A lot of people who experience the things you are, wish they didn't. The visions can be disturbing and get in the way of normal life. But I'm afraid this is a gift you've been given. There is no way to get rid of it."

"So the things I'm seeing are real events that are taking place?"

"In the cases I've studied, yes. From what Barbara tells me, you've been a witness to some pretty disturbing things."

"Murder. I guess that's about as terrifying as you can get. But in one of the visions, the killer saw me, and I'm worried he's going to—"

"Find you?"

"Yes."

"That's not possible. Remember, you're the one experiencing the phenomenon, not the person who might see you. It just means your extrasensory perceptions are so strong something like that can occasionally happen. What is taking place with you is rare. I've studied a few cases in which this was the finding. Not many, but a handful."

"I just can't deal with it."

"A big part of this is acceptance. It is who you are. And it's okay. We all have our gifts and talents, yours just happens to be clairvoyance. You know, I had a difficult time with mine too."

"So you're—"

She nodded. "Yes. That's the main reason I got into studying it. I needed a deeper understanding, and there just wasn't a lot of scientific acceptance out there concerning the paranormal at the time. But now, there are quite a few major scientists and doctors conducting research into this and having successful results. We have come a long way."

"Thank you, professor, for taking the time to come here to see me."

She stood, taking a business card out of her purse, and handing it to Jenna. "Please call me if you have any questions, or just want to talk. I'm here for you. The best advice I can give you, and what helped me the most, is when I stopped being afraid of it. When I decided to do that, my life changed for the better. You will learn to live with it. Embrace your gifts instead of fearing them. You'll see what I'm talking about. Everything is going to be okay, trust me."

Jenna couldn't describe the relief washing over her. For the first time since this whole thing started, she was more at peace.

After the two women showed the professor out, Barbara turned to Jenna with a glare on her face. "What do you think?"

"Well, I had every intention to kill you for inviting that lady here without telling me."

Her friend stood there with crossed arms. "And what would you have said if I'd have warned you ahead of time?"

"I would have never opened the door."

"Exactly."

Chapter Five

After the long trip back to Farmersville, the killer finally pulled onto the dirt path leading into the woods to an abandoned hay barn. He used this place before and was confident no one would ever find it.

His latest prey was still out cold in the backseat. He'd gather all the tools he needed for playtime, then make the necessary preparations before waking her.

He grabbed the duffel bag of goodies out of the trunk and headed toward the old, ramshackle building. He made his way to the shelf and lit the lantern. His attention slid over the gray blanket he'd left spread out on the floor from the last visit. Good. Less work to do before getting to the reason he came here.

The shackles were a different story. Those couldn't very well be left behind in the event someone managed to stumble onto this place. If they saw them, they'd damn well be suspicious there had been some nefarious goings-on here. And the police would be crawling all over the place.

Escaping capture for this long hadn't come without being extra smart and cautious. He was much wiser than any of them gave him credit for. If they'd only known the truth about the ultimate scheme he had managed to pull off years ago, then they would know without a doubt they were dealing with the most clever serial killer in all of history. At times, it had been a challenge to keep quiet about it.

He removed the chains and handcuffs from the bag, arranging them so the girl's hands would hang from the rafters. Now for the shackles to hold her legs in place. Picturing the expression on the bitch's face when he woke her, and she realized the depth of the terrifying situation afoot was an electrifying thought. The reactions of his victims were always the same, weren't they? At first, fear would take over and she'd cry and beg him not to kill her. Then she'd be fooled into believing cooperation would spare her life. By the time reality set in, and it became obvious death was the only ending, she'd whimper like a spineless coward. When he finished with her, she would consider him ending her life as quickly as possible an act of kindness.

He made the final preparations by setting out the makeup. Dolling her up would be one of his favorite parts. Now that the stage was set, the time had come to present the star of the show.

She lay there in the backseat of the car quiet and at peace. His victim's black hair spilling over the ivory tone of her arm was a picture-worthy sight. It stirred something deep inside him to see her this way. After tonight, the little bitch would never be this undisturbed again. The time had come to get on with it. He was bursting with excitement and had waited long enough.

He carried her into the barn and dumped the body onto the blanket like a sack of potatoes, hoping the action would rouse her, but she was still out cold.

It would be a better experience if she fought him like a wildcat as he undressed her and got the shackles on. The smelling salts in the bag would wake her. Never mind. There'd be plenty of time to have his fun once he completed the task at hand.

She moaned a bit as he cut off her clothes using a pair of shears. "Relax, sweet-cheeks," he said, finishing the job and grabbing the shackles, "we haven't even gotten to the good part yet."

With the manacles now fastened to her ankles, he lifted the girl against the wall and snapped on the handcuffs. She stirred, and his excitement grew.

Her eyes opened, and he counted down the seconds, one, two, three, until, at last, they grew wide with fear. "Who…who are you?"

She jerked against the cuffs. Chains rattled—music to his ears—as she struggled against her bonds.

C'mon, bitch, let it out.

Here came the scream, a loud pitched sound that sent him into a dance. He threw up his hands as if holding a baton and conducting the rise and fall of her shrill cries like an orchestra. Then he suddenly stopped, and got in her face quickly, saying, "Go ahead, scream your little head off. No one can hear you."

"Please…just let me go. Don't hurt me."

He smiled big. "Oh, I'm going to hurt you. But I might let you go if you do exactly what I say."

Tears ran down her face, leaving black streaks of mascara as she sobbed uncontrollably.

He clicked his tongue. "Come now. You're messing up your pretty face, and we can't have that."

"Wh…what do you w…want me to do?"

"We're going to pretty you up, and play a little game, okay?"

****

Jason Cheng arrived a few minutes past eight p.m. Channing showed him into Cole's office.

The Asian kid couldn't have been more than five feet tall. He was thin and well dressed, with a pair of thick-rimmed glasses. Cole stood and introduced himself, and then gestured for the young man to sit down. "I know it's late," he said, "I appreciate you coming in like this."

"No problem. Jessica told me you would probably be calling."

"How is she, by the way?"

He frowned and leaned back in the chair. "A little shaken up, but I think she's going to be okay."

"Good. I'm glad to hear it."

"So who is this guy that tried to attack her?"

"That's what we're trying to find out. Jessica said he offered her a ride earlier in the night when you arrived to pick her up."

"Yes. There was someone parked by the curb where she was waiting. When I pulled up, the guy left quickly. Jessica later told me he had been trying to give her a ride. She seemed relieved I got there when I did."

"Can you describe the car he was driving?"

"Sure. Looked like a light brown, 1970s Gremlin. The back bumper was silver with quite a few rust spots. It was banged up."

It was a longshot to ask, but… "Did you happen to catch the license plate number?"

"I can remember the first few digits."

Cole expressed optimism. Although the entire plate number would have been better, with a partial, they could compile a register of similar automobiles in the area matching the kid's description. It would take some time to run down the list, but a promising start was what they needed. "Did you see the guy?"

"I wish I would have paid more attention, honestly. If I had known…"

Cole hadn't run across many people who were that perceptive to their surroundings, especially when they didn't realize they may be a witness to the things they saw. "Anything else you noticed that might be important?"

Jason shrugged, appearing apologetic, and then thought better of it. "Well, wait. I remember seeing a bumper sticker on the rear window."

Cole perked up. "Great."

"The color was brown with white lettering. An army sticker of some kind. You could tell it had been there a while."

That would make the vehicle stand out from others. He ripped off a post-a-note from the top of the pile and handed it to the kid along with a pencil. "Why don't you write down what you remember of the license plate?"

Just then commotion stirred outside the office. Before Cole could figure out what might be the cause, Jenna bounded into the room, Channing on her heels. The detective threw up his hands. "I tried to tell her you were with someone right now."

To say she was upset would have been an understatement. "I've got this," Cole said, dismissing the detective and gesturing for Jenna to have a seat. He encouraged Jason to finish the task, and then took the paper, issuing a thank you.

The kid strolled out and shut the door.

From the appearance of her, she'd just seen a ghost. "What's wrong?"

"I had a vision of another kidnapping. The girl is

being held hostage in an old barn. She's still alive."

"Where?"

"I don't know. But I feel it's close by."

He leaned across his desk, frustrated. "That doesn't help, Jenna. You can't give me a location. Exactly what am I supposed to do with this information?"

She stood, eyes widening in exasperation. "Go look for the girl before he kills her."

"I can't do that when I don't know where she is."

Desperation clung to her expression. "You could at least try."

"Give me something to go on."

"Jesus Christ, it's only a matter of time before that monster murders her."

He closed his eyes and sighed. "Sit down for a minute. I need you to think. What did you see?"

"We don't have time for—"

"Jenna, please."

Searching his expression, she finally sat. But still appeared exhausted and restless at the same time. "I've seen the girl in handcuffs hanging from rafters. There are shackles on her ankles. He puts makeup on his victims. It's part of some sick game. She's so scared." Tears streamed down her face as she said, "He is sexually assaulting her in ways you just couldn't imagine."

For the first time, Cole got a glimpse of raw emotion coming from her he hadn't seen before. Jenna was deeply disturbed by what she'd witnessed. Even the best actress would have a hard time pulling off something that genuine without the skills to back it up. And as far as he knew, she'd never taken acting classes. "Tell me about the surroundings."

He could tell she was working toward enough composure to tap into her memory. "This isn't the first time he's been there," Jenna said, closing her eyes, concentrating. "He's held other women captive in the same place. I see a gray blanket on the ground. And a duffel bag. Items spread out. Scissors, a pair of pliers, a knife. Blood on the cover. The girl is bleeding."

"Where, Jenna? Tell me where it is."

She opened her eyes, and disappointment emanated from them. "I can't…I can only see the inside."

Where had he heard that before? That's exactly what she had to say about Sylvia Clark's murderer. *I saw the inside of his house.* It's quite suspicious the woman could never seem to identify anything outside, something that might give them an inkling as to where to search. She almost had him fooled this time. How much thicker could she have poured it on? What a hopeless idiot he was.

"Go home, Jenna," he said, between gritted teeth.

"You have to do something."

"What?" He leapt out of his chair, eyes pinning her to the seat. "Will you have me send a dozen helicopters to search every field within a thirty-mile radius? Should I gather a hundred men and twenty dogs to comb the backyard of every citizen in this town? Will that do?"

"You're just going to let her die?"

"I need real clues. Practical leads. Not this cockamamie crap you've been giving me. You are not helping to solve this case. All you're doing is making yourself look guilty as hell. I suggest you talk to an attorney before coming back in here."

She stood and got in his face. "You are no detective, Cole Rainwater. If you were, you'd give a shit about saving lives. You are far too hung up on technicalities to recognize help when you see it. I am done with you."

"That's the best news I've heard all day!"

The door slammed.

****

The killer checked the time on his phone before pulling away from the barn. It was six a.m. Raping, beating, and torturing that little bitch for almost ten hours set a record. By the time it was over, he had been too exhausted to strangle her, let alone move the body. Doing so would have made him late for work. After taking the week off due to his boss being out of town, today a timely arrival was expected.

To make things easier, he'd administered a high dose of roofies. That much of the date rape drug was supposed to stop her breathing—and in this case it worked. He'd checked before leaving. Now the only thing required would be for him to come back at the end of the day to dispose of the body.

But there was one duty left to take care of before arriving on the jobsite. He couldn't continue to take the risk someone saw his vehicle in connection with the girl who got away. Getting rid of the car would have been done yesterday if it hadn't been for the desperate need to feed his hunger. Now that that was out of the way, things should get back on track again. He'd built in enough time to handle the vehicle situation and hitchhike the rest of the way to his destination if need be. The perfect spot to take the car came to mind. He'd have to get a move on though.

Fifteen minutes down the road, he pulled off the highway and onto a side road. After passing a handful of houses spaced far apart, a dirt trail came into view. The path would lead farther back into the woods. The passageway ended a few miles in and opened into a forest. He maneuvered between trees and over the heavy brush until arriving at a small clearing. This place was deserted, and no one would come out here before the opening day of dove hunting season, and that wouldn't be until September, six months away. These woods were as familiar as the back of his hands, and he already had a route picked out that would get him to the highway where a ride could be flagged down.

He killed the engine, got out, and retrieved the gas can in the trunk. After removing the duffle bag and anything inside the car that could link him to it, he stripped off both the front and back license plates. Couldn't have the authorities tracing the vehicle back to the original owner. Next, he doused the interior with gasoline and splashed the rest on the tires and roof. He struck a match and tossed it through the open window.

He waited until the blaze became an inferno before unzipping the bag and stuffing the license plates inside. It was time to go.

The last time he hitchhiked had been after the Gulf War. Upon coming home from the service in Kuwait, he thumbed his way from the army base all the way back to Farmersville just to surprise his wife and son who hadn't seen him in over four months.

Truth be told, the demons inside had reared their heads during that damn war. They hadn't subsided upon returning home. They only festered, offering a full picture of what he was. Knowing gave him the courage to commit all the vile acts he had been foolish enough to suppress all those years. Accepting the monster inside meant beloved freedom to act on his desires. Too bad things ended the way they had though. It would have been badass if his demons and family could have coexisted with one another. But with this kind of gift, holding on to loved ones was a false hope. It had been a lesson learned long ago.

By the time he made it to the highway and stuck out his thumb, it took no more than five minutes for a car to pull off onto the shoulder.

As he approached the driver, a man who appeared to be in his early twenties stuck his head out the window. "You need a ride?"

He peered inside and saw the driver was alone. Perfect. "Oh, man, that'd be great."

"Well, jump in."

"Thanks." The killer made strides to the other side of the car.

The stranger pointed over his shoulder. "Just put your bag in the back seat."

After doing what the driver suggested, he opened the door and slid in. "I appreciate you stopping. My car broke down back there." Before making a final decision to act on impulse, kill the man, and take off with his car, he needed to prod for additional information. "Heading to work this morning?"

He shook his head. "Going through a divorce right now. Had to sell my house. I'm heading to Louisiana for a new job opportunity. A fresh start, ya know."

"Leaving Texas, huh?"

"Yeah. At least for a while. Sometimes you gotta get away."

"You from around here?"

"Nope, just passing through."

The stars just aligned in his favor. "Tell you what, if you can take me a few blocks that way," he said, pointing straight ahead, "I have a buddy who lives here in town, and he can help get my car started."

"Sure thing."

Now for part two of the plan. "It's right up here, on the left," he said, quietly slipping the pocketknife out of the front pocket of his jeans.

As the driver took the turn, he said, "This is some beautiful country out here."

He was in no mood for small talk. The guy would be dead in about another minute or two anyhow. *That's it, just a little farther.* "Right here."

The man stopped the car, peering out the window. "Are you sure? I don't see a house."

"That's because there isn't one." The second the stranger faced him he plunged the knife into his throat.

Blood spilled down the front of the guy's shirt and he jerked erratically, hands going to his neck. But it was too late. The killer stared dead into the eyes of the man as he gasped for air.

Die, you bastard, and stop wasting my time. Life drained from the stranger's eyes, and then the killer plucked the weapon from his throat. He wiped off the blood-smeared blade on the front of the guy's shirt, folded the knife, and stuck it back in his pocket.

He sprinted quickly around to the driver's side and hauled the guy from the car. After dragging the body further into the woods, he was careful to check the man's pockets to remove any identification. The car needed to be used as long as possible, and it would take authorities at least a week to figure out who this guy was by the time they found the corpse, especially if no one reported him missing right away. And he was sure they wouldn't.

But as he headed to the car, an idea struck him. Another set of license plates would keep the heat at bay even longer, and the perfect spot to get them came to mind. He took the phone out of his pocket and checked the time. Acting quickly should give him enough time to put the plan into action and make it to work without being late.

He jumped in the car and headed straight for the nearest gas station. Approaching the store, he slowed. The deserted parking lot brought a smile to his face. It was early. The sun hadn't come up yet, and customers weren't out and about.

As he killed the headlights and turned into the store from the side entrance, what must have been the clerk's car was parked toward the end of the lot. Better than expected. The employee's vehicle appeared to be the same make and model as the one he just stole. What were the odds? The fortunate events paving the way for him to obtain everything needed ever since he took that little bitch hostage last night, must have been a sign from the gods his life had a bigger significance than ever imagined.

After pulling up next to the car, he turned off the ignition and rummaged around in the glove box for a screwdriver. And sure enough, he found one, further cementing his belief he was on the right track to something truly spiritual.

He unscrewed both license plates from the stolen car as quickly as possible and carried them around to the clerk's car, unscrewing those as well, and switched them out. Once the task was complete, he jumped back into the dead man's car and took off.

He turned on the radio, tuned it to his favorite station, and whistled along with the song pouring out of the speakers.

It was going to be a hell of a day.

****

Grinning like a kid on Christmas morning, Gibbs placed a few sheets of paper on Cole's desk. "There's only seventeen male registered drivers within a fifty-mile radius matching the vehicle description and the partial plate number."

Cole snatched the papers off his desk and examined the list, searching the names to see if any of them stood out.

Gibbs said, "There's two on the list that have priors. One is serving a six-year sentence for robbery. But the other," he added, pointing to a name midway down the list, "is a registered sex offender in Collin County, released from state prison last year."

Cole shuffled to the next page and stared at the hardened face of a middle-aged man with a ponytail and goatee. The name at the top of the page was Seth Middleton. He recalled Jenna's description. *He has a goatee.* Butterflies developed in his stomach. Could this be their man? Would it be this easy?

"Channing is headed out right now to bring the guy in for questioning."

A few seconds later, commotion stirred in the bullpen. "Get your hands off me. You have no right to do this."

He and Gibbs stepped out of the office. The man in the photo wrestled with two officers holding him on either side. "I want to talk to my attorney. This is harassment. I have rights, ya know."

"Relax," Channing told the guy. "We're investigating a crime, and we just have a few questions."

"Fuck your questions. Am I being detained, or am I free to go?"

"You're not under arrest. We'll just get a search warrant for your house and your truck. Oh, and I'll need to contact your place of employment too. We need to have a chat with them, ya know, for the sake of our investigation. Or you can just answer our questions. But you're free to go." Channing instructed the officers who had him by the arms, to release the guy.

Middleton appeared as angry as a bull, ready to charge. But in less than a minute he relented. It wasn't as if they left him much choice. "What do you want?"

Channing said, "Come with me." He led the guy into the interrogation room. "Have a seat. We'll be right with you."

Cole was right outside the door, waiting. "Did you find him at home?"

Channing shook his head. "I tracked him down at work."

Cole imagined that scene. "No wonder he's so pissed. You going to question the suspect yourself, or do you want some assistance?"

"Let me have a crack at him first. If I need backup, I'll call for you," Channing stepped through the door and shut it.

As Cole headed to his office, a phone rang somewhere in the department. He no sooner made it to the desk than Beckett rushed in. "A girl has been found in shackles inside an old hay barn located south about ten miles off the highway. It's in the field behind the water tower. We're not sure what shape she's in. But she's alive. The medics are on their way now."

Cole grabbed his keys off his desk. "Someone get word to Channing."

After meeting up with his partner out in the bullpen, they both left together and rushed to the scene.

Pulling up at the location, Cole spotted one of the forensic technicians he was familiar with talking to a tall man standing off to the side of the barn. As soon as he and Gibbs stepped from the car, the technician noticed their arrival, exchanged some words with the man, and they both headed in his direction.

"This is Sean Walker," the tech said, "He owns the property and is the one who found the vic. I figured you'd want to talk to him." He nodded, excusing himself. "I've got to get back inside. They are about to transport her."

Gibbs disappeared inside while Cole introduced himself to the witness. "Hi, Mr. Walker, I'm Detective Rainwater with the Farmersville PD." He put out a hand, and the guy shook it. "What time did you stumble across the woman in your hay barn?"

"Oh gosh." Cole could see he was disturbed by what he'd seen; he was almost ashen. "I got here about fifteen minutes ago. I was walking the property when I heard faint moans coming from inside. I went in, and there she was, hanging from the rafters. I couldn't believe it."

"What do you mean, hanging from the rafters?"

"She was handcuffed to a chain up there," he said, pointing toward the sky. "Her legs were shackled. She wasn't moving, just groaning sorta. That's the only way

I could tell she was still alive. Then I immediately called 911."

"When was the last time you were out here?"

"About ten years ago. The only reason I came today is because I'm getting ready to put this property on the market and I'm supposed to meet the surveyor here in about thirty minutes."

"You'll need to put that off for now. This is a crime scene, and we'll need access to the property for further investigations."

"I understand completely." The guy put his hands in his pockets and stared at the ground, shaking his head. "What kind of sick bastard would do something like that to someone?"

"We plan on finding out. Has there been anyone else on your property you're aware of?"

"No. Well, besides the occasional hunter, I guess."

"So you haven't given anyone permission to hunt on your land or be here for any reason?"

"No."

"I'm going to leave you with a business card, Mr. Walker. If you think of anything you feel would be important to tell us, please give me a call. And I may get in touch with you later if I have additional questions for you." Cole handed a business card over and then flipped open his memo pad, pen poised over the paper. "Go ahead and give me your number."

After writing it down, he wandered over to Gibbs, who stood outside the barn, staring down at something. He glanced at Cole. "Does that look like a tire impression to you?"

Cole took a closer examination, seeing a clear print in the dirt resembling what Gibbs mentioned. "Get on the phone with the department. We need someone here to take a cast now."

"I'm on it," Gibbs said, grabbing his phone.

Cole faced the barn. The EMTs were just now wheeling the victim out on a stretcher. He followed behind them as they headed toward the waiting ambulance, and asked, "What shape is she in?

The one on the right with the curly, red hair answered. "She's been beaten within an inch of her life. We're pretty sure she's been drugged. She is slipping in and out of consciousness. But her pulse is strong, which is a good sign."

"What hospital are you taking her to?"

"McKinney Medical Center."

Cole wandered back to Gibbs, deciding he should be the one to visit the hospital. If anyone could talk to her, he wanted to be the one to do it.

Gibbs said, "They're sending Henderson here to take the cast."

Cole pointed to the barn and asked, "Forensics done processing yet?"

"Nope. Still in there."

"What do you think?"

Gibbs frowned, the expression in his eyes full of uncertainty. "Honestly, we are going to have to wait and see what they come up with. There's a lot of hay on the ground in there. The chances are slim of lifting a clear shoe print."

"We need to talk to the girl."

"From the looks of her, that may be a while."

Cole wondered about Channing's progress with the sex offender they had been questioning at the precinct when him and Gibbs left. But he couldn't be at two places at once. It would be best to be at the hospital with the victim more than anything else.

"When we get back to the station, why don't you see how far Channing has gotten with our person of interest, and I'm going to head to the hospital to see if I can talk to the victim."

"All right, then. Let's get the hell out of here."

Chapter Six

Thank God for a lunch break.

The killer headed for his car. Having been up all night left him exhausted. A shower would be great, not to mention a bite to eat. But there was no time for either. Earlier, he'd made the decision to head out to the hay barn and dispose of the girl's body in the afternoon instead of the end of the day.

But for some strange reason, he'd been feeling antsy. He'd left the bitch as dead as a doornail, and there were serious doubts anyone would wander out there, he didn't like the feeling of loose ends dangling in the wind, even if it was for only a couple hours.

Jumping in the car and taking off, he questioned his way of doing things. Being this sloppy wasn't cutting it. And lately, the thirst for violence had begun to overshadow good sense. Starting today, though, that would change. And he'd kick it off with taking a break from killing. Even if it was only for a month.

He needed to back away and let the dust settle for a while. The murders being so close together only increased the chances of getting caught. Even though he'd been on one of the best thrill rides of his life, if he didn't slow down, it would be over for good. He nodded to himself and turned onto the highway ramp. Somehow he'd suffer through the reprieve; it was necessary.

Once reaching Farmersville and no longer able to fend off the hunger pains, he pulled into a convenience store and purchased a bag of chips and a soda. He was back on the road in no time and heading toward the water tower.

He ascended the hill just before the turnoff, surprised to see flashing lights in the distance. Rounding the curve, squad cars were as plain as the nose on his face. Three of them, blocking off the road leading to the hay barn. He slowed the car with a pounding heart. A state trooper stood on the side of the highway, directing traffic around the blockade.

Everything in his gut told him they'd found her.

How was that possible? He'd been sure he left her dead. She wasn't breathing, right? If the bitch survived, there'd be no way she could break out of her bonds and make it to the highway for help. The barn sat a good mile back into the woods, isolated from everything.

Someone had to find her. But who? The place hadn't been used in years. How could the police know she had been there? And more importantly, had they found the girl alive? She'd seen his face.

He drove on past, going about a mile or two up the road, and then turned into the empty parking lot of a church. He needed to breathe, pull himself together. Stop panicking. The more time spent sitting here, the wilder the scenarios were forming in his mind. That old, familiar feeling of the police closing in on him was back, and it crushed him like an insect. But if he didn't calm down, he would faint from hyperventilating.

Perhaps it wasn't that bad. Maybe someone hunting for wild hogs found the girl, and she was already dead. The best thing to do would be to go home and turn on the news. To hell with work. There'd be no possible way he could concentrate on the job anyhow. He'd call his boss, make up some believable excuse, then head to the house.

Mind made up, he left the parking lot and grabbed his phone. What started as a great day had taken a surprising turn, like a rollercoaster barreling straight toward the gates of hell.

****

Cole got up and peered out the window overlooking the hospital parking lot. He'd been sitting in the waiting room going on two and a half hours when a physician appeared inside the door.

Cole approached him. "How is she, Doc?"

"She's sustained multiple fractures, including a broken clavicle—the collar bone—as well as some pretty serious cuts, bruising, and swelling. We were able to confirm she was drugged. There was a high enough dose of Rohypnol in her system to stop her respirations permanently. The girl is lucky to be alive."

"The date rape drug?"

"Yes. We have given her an antidote intravenously and transferred her to the ICU for close monitoring."

"So does it look like she's out of the woods?"

"There's a long road to recovery ahead of her, Detective. It's not just the physical injuries. The mental abuse will cause a much more long-term effect."

"I understand, Doctor. Was a rape kit performed?"

"I was informed that was addressed in the ER."

"When do you think she'll be able to talk to us?"

"I realize your need to question the patient. But her well-being is my number one priority."

This wasn't the first time Cole had to deal with

doctors in connection with injured witnesses. Although their job entailed protecting their patients, his involved protecting the public. Speaking with surviving victims was every bit as important to a detective as collecting clues. In this case, if he couldn't question her in a timely manner, this girl would not be the only patient the doctor would be looking after. If future victims were lucky enough to be looked at.

"The animal who did this to your patient has recently murdered other women over a matter of weeks. This girl might hold the key to his identity. I'm going to need to speak to her as soon as she is awake."

"You realize one of the side effects of Rohypnol is a loss of memory. She may not recall the attack."

"I'll take my chances."

The doctor stared at Cole for a moment too long, and Cole could tell he cared nothing about compliance. What the guy thought mattered little to him. More important was whether he was granted access to a witness that could very well lead to the arrest of a monster running around killing innocent women.

The doctor gave an annoyed sigh. "Very well then. As soon as she awakens, I'll have one of the nurses call you. Just leave a card at the front desk."

As the physician strode off, Cole's cell phone rang. Gibbs' contact popped up. "What have you got?"

"The sex offender is a dead end."

He should have known it was too good to be true. "What happened?"

"His alibis checked out. The guy works nights, and the boss has put him there every night from ten p.m. to eight a.m., Monday through Saturday. He says Middleton hasn't missed a day in eight months.

According to the ME's reported time of death, he couldn't have committed any of the murders."

Just like that, back to square one. "Any news on the identity of the girl yet?"

"Yep. We just got word about fifteen minutes ago. Meant to call you, but things have been crazy here running down alibis, and following up with the names on the list of registered car owners."

"Have you gotten anywhere on that?"

"Hell no. We are winding our way down the list. Nothing promising yet."

"Okay, what about the identity of the girl?"

"Her name is Gloria Perez. Her fiancé was watching the news and thought the kidnap victim might have been her after she went missing last night. Turns out he was right."

"Who is the fiancé?"

"No one of interest I don't think. They have a house together in Whitney. He reported her missing last night after he got home from work, saw the car in the driveway, door open, and her purse spilled out on the floorboard."

"Whitney? That's a little over a two-hour drive from here."

"Yeah, I think so."

Cole considered something he hadn't before. "Maybe we should reach out to other counties for reports of missing persons or unsolved homicides. If our guy is going all the way to Whitney, there's no telling where else he's been."

"I am on it. Did you ever get to talk to the girl?"

"Not yet. I talked to the doctor though. It sounds like she'll pull through. I think our guy tried to kill her with an overdose of the date rape drug. He probably figured the girl was dead before he took off."

"Well, if he had planned on coming back to move her body, no one's shown up yet. We've got eyes out there, and there's been no report of his vehicle anywhere around that place."

"Hmm. He's been pretty good about burning the bodies to destroy DNA. It doesn't make sense he'd intentionally leave her there."

"No, but he could have seen it on the news. That would have been a tip-off."

"That's true. Let's go ahead and put an officer outside her room. There's a good chance she's seen the perp's face. And if that's the case, I don't want to risk him coming to the hospital to finish the job."

"I can do that. Oh, and I wanted to let you know Jenna's here. She stopped by to see you."

What now?

She had come into his office last night, and yet again, forewarned him about a victim they were going to find. That earned him a massive headache, trying to figure out how she could know about these crimes before the cops did. It would be easy to connect the dots and determine Jenna's involvement.

But he knew her, and no part of him could believe she was a psychopathic killer. There was no way she'd have the stomach to commit something like that or stand by and watch someone else do it.

"What's up with you guys?" Gibbs asked, snapping him out of his preoccupation.

"What do you mean?"

"You two know each other?"

Cole was in no mood to explain the sordid past he

shared with Jenna to his partner—let alone anyone else. Things between them were complicated enough without dragging other people into it.

"That's none of your business."

"Is she a witness or something?"

"No." *Just drop it, man.*

"Well, the way she was talking the other day—"

"Enough with the twenty questions, man. She's not a witness."

"You know what I think?"

"Don't care."

"I think you're attracted to her."

"What?"

"Don't tell me you haven't noticed how hot she is. If you don't plan to ask her out, I was thinking—"

"The hell you are."

"Aha! I knew you liked her. Why aren't you doing anything about it?"

"You don't know what the hell you're talking about."

"Did you guys date or something?"

"We are done with this conversation."

"Whatever you say, partner. I just wish you trusted me enough to talk to me."

"Thanks for the therapy session. I'll see you back at the precinct." He got off the phone, much more agitated now than he had been all damned day.

If he'd thought things couldn't get any worse, after the twenty-five-minute drive back to the police station, it did. The moment he stepped through the door, the sound of Jenna's laughter spilled out from the direction of Gibbs' office.

He headed straight for the room and entered just as

Gibbs was grinning like a Cheshire cat. His attention slid over Jenna sitting there, seemingly delighted by their little chat. The smile melted right off her face the second their eyes met.

Gibbs on the other hand appeared as if he was enjoying himself even more now that Cole showed up. "Well, hey there, partner. Me and Jenna here were just getting acquainted. She's got some amusing stories about the two of you when you were teenagers."

Cole just knew if the color in his face matched the fury swelling inside, it would be fire engine red. He stalked off, slamming the door behind him.

The creaking of the door, and the high heels clicking across the floor told him Jenna was in pursuit. "Cole, wait," she said, as he continued toward his office, ignoring her.

"Did you hear me? What's wrong with you?" She caught up with him as he rounded the corner. "Stop, will you?"

He kept walking. "Go back to Gibbs' office. You seemed pretty cozy in there."

"Are you jealous?

He stopped dead in his tracks, turned and glared at her. "Of what? We haven't slept together since we were in high school."

Cole instinctively glanced around, noticing at least ten people out in the bullpen who stopped what they were doing to watch them. The place suddenly became silent enough to hear a pin drop. And that never happened. *Well, shit.* He plodded into his office and shut the door.

Jenna knocked.

He acted like he didn't hear it.

She stepped in. “I’m sorry. I shouldn’t have said that.”

He stood behind his chair, gripping the back of it, holding on to the last bit of control he had left. Seeing her beautiful face day after day was getting to him, and he damned well knew it. “What exactly do you want?”

“I heard about the girl who was found today.”

“You came all the way here for that? You could have watched it on the news. So what are you doing here?”

Peering down, she appeared lost for words. And then, “The guy who kidnapped her set his car on fire.”

He smirked, refusing to meet her eyes. “Let me guess, another famous vision, right?”

“I know where it is this time.”

“Well, isn’t that noble? Are the psychic gods giving you locations now?”

“I can take you there.”

He frowned, making a show of considering her offer. “Tell you what, I’ll take time out of my busy day from trying to catch a killer to take a joyride with you, if for no other reason than to show you how insane this is. But when we come back empty-handed, this nonsense stops. Agreed?”

She dodged his eyes by staring at the ground, saying nothing.

He didn’t let her get away with it. “Jenna?”

“Fine,” she said, meeting his gaze at last.

He stepped around and opened the door, moving aside for her to exit first. “Then let’s go.”

****

The killer no sooner hit the door of his house than he rushed into the living room and turned on the TV.

Flipping through channels, he finally ran across the local news. And there it was in all its glory, the scene of the earlier murder.

He stared at the hay barn, squad cars surrounding the place, police everywhere. Three EMTs wheeled a stretcher out, heading toward an ambulance, as the newscaster told the tale of a twenty-two-year-old victim with multiple injuries being taken to McKinney Medical Center for treatment.

He cursed, picked up an empty glass on the coffee table, and threw it against the wall. The shattering sound sliced right through him. The bad omen that occurred years ago, was happening all over again. Just like the last time. Recklessness and letting his guard down allowed them to get closer. And if he wasn't careful, they'd swarm him like an army of ants and take him apart, piece by piece.

Who found the bitch?

As the scene continued to unfold, it didn't take long before the answer was clear. The property owner, who hadn't stepped foot on the land in years, decided to put it up for sale. And today of all days, he'd gone there to meet the surveyor. What a bizarre set of circumstances.

But what the news reporter said next caused the blood to drain from his face. She described the suspect's car, along with the mention of an army sticker on the back window.

Thank God I got rid of the damn thing.

But how the hell did they know the make and model? He sat on the couch, face buried in his hands, thinking. Then it hit him…the one who got away. His premonition had been right about that. He had tried to pick the girl up earlier in the night, right? Yes, but she didn't get a good look at him when he attempted to kidnap her hours later. Didn't matter. Once the police started questioning their victim, it probably wouldn't have taken much to put two and two together.

He had bigger problems. Although she didn't see his face, the one he'd left for dead, who was now lying in the hospital, had. What could he do? It wasn't like he could just march into that place and take her out. They'd have someone standing guard outside the bitch's room. No one was getting near her.

"Shit!"

He liked this place and his job. Packing up and leaving would be a hassle. What about the disguises? He had a box of different wigs, glasses, a few mustaches, and beards in the closet. Hell, if memory served correct, there were still a few colored contacts from the good old days. But those things were a pain in the ass when they had to be used the last time. He'd had it good for so long. And now?

Glancing at the TV, something caught his attention. He grabbed the remote and hit rewind. Thirty seconds in, a figure shifted across the screen again. Clicking pause froze the frame. There, over the shoulder of the reporter standing in front of the Farmersville PD, was a small woman entering the double doors of the precinct. He pushed play for another three seconds, until the lady turned around, facing the camera. Pausing it again and staring at her, he wondered why she was so familiar.

And then it dawned on him. He got up and stood directly in front of the screen to get a closer look.

Holy shit. That can't be her.

****

Having Jenna sitting beside Cole in his truck again after ten years couldn't have been more surreal. They had spent so many summers right here in this vehicle, heading out to the beach in Galveston, to the old drive-in theater off Main Street, and cruising to the football games on Friday night. The weekends of partying with friends in the middle of cow pastures, the tailgate dropped, sipping on moonshine while they gazed at the stars. The many nights they had snuck off and made love on this very seat. Back then he figured they'd be together forever. It never dawned on him tragedy would strike, and their affair would all be over so quickly.

But here they were. All grown up and having been away from each other for so long. Cole closed his eyes for just a second against the pain of what could have been. He could never get that time back with her. The opportunity was lost as if it were a ship at sea swallowed up in the thick of fog. He glanced at her, taking a snapshot in his mind of how she was, sitting there. When Jenna left Texas for the second time, breaking his heart all over again, he would carry that memory with him for the next ten years.

"It's just up ahead," she said, snapping him back to the present.

Although many of the county roads connected, like a giant grid, they were headed in a direction familiar to him. "Take a right on the next road."

When he made the turn, it wasn't yet clear if she was leading them to the place he remembered. But as she told him to make a left at the end of the street, it was apparent they were headed to the spot in the woods where they used to make out when they were teenagers. He stopped the truck. What kind of sick game was this?

"What are you doing?"

He reversed. "We're going back."

"What? Why?"

"You know why."

"Cole, stop. Please."

He threw the gearshift in park and faced her. "I can't take this shit anymore, Jenna. It isn't enough you walked out on me when I needed you the most. But now you've come back and you're doing everything you can to torture me. Do you know how devastated I was when you left? Do you have any idea what kind of hell my nights were? I did everything I could to forget you, but it was never enough. Why are you trying so hard to get back at me by taking me here?"

She sat there, mouth open. The expression in her eyes, a reflection of torment. "Believe me when I say this place holds as many painful memories for me as it does for you. My intention is not to hurt you. And it never has been. The only reason I was able to recognize this spot when I had my vision, is because I saw our names carved in the oak tree."

"The hits just keep coming with you."

"If there's nothing there," she said, pointing ahead, beyond the tall weeds, "I'll do what you want. I'll leave you alone, and I won't bother you with this ever again. You have my word."

Gazing out the windshield, a decision churned in his mind. Truth be told, he didn't want her to leave him alone. Ever since she'd returned, he was alive again for the first time since she'd left. But a reprieve from the madness the woman had been wreaking on him, would be nice.

He put the vehicle in drive and eased his foot on

the accelerator without saying a word. After maneuvering carefully around trees, the outline of a large object took shape up ahead in the clearing.

The burnt body of the car they had been searching for sat about ten feet in front of him. And the tree with their names on it was so close to the window he could reach out and touch it. The words shot an arrow through his heart:

Jenna and Cole, forever.

Chapter Seven

Jenna stepped out of the shower, recalling the expression in Cole's eyes as he poured his heart out to her in the truck. Since being back in Texas, she had yet to see him so vulnerable. It was a wonder if he still cared about her at all and ever really did.

Now it was clear he must have, to have been that affected by her leaving. Given the choice, she'd go back, beg her parents not to go, do whatever needed to be done to keep them in Texas.

If she'd only known the truth.

Would it have changed anything? Absolutely. If Cole had been there, they would have run away together before allowing her parents to take her. That was how much she loved him.

But it was water over the damn now, wasn't it? That scene already played out, and the outcome had fundamentally changed everything. When and if he found out her secret, it would drive him away for good. The best thing to do would be to pack up and go back to Georgia just as soon as the business deal finished. He would never understand the decision Amanda Langley forced her to make back then. And Jenna couldn't blame him.

Telling Cole the truth before leaving was only fair. She owed him that much. But she couldn't even imagine how to go about doing it.

While dressing, the doorbell rang. She patted her hair dry and headed for the door.

The sun was setting behind Cole, leaning against the doorway, his arms crossed in front of him. Like he was on a mission.

She left the door ajar, and sat on the couch, continuing to dry her hair.

He lumbered over and stood in front of her. "I'm sorry."

"For what?"

"Not believing you." He cleared his throat, putting off the impression that he realized how much of a jackass he was. "I've done a little research, talked to a few people, and it seems, perhaps, I was a little judgmental about this whole clairvoyant thing."

She swallowed, laying the towel across the arm of the couch. "I guess I can't blame you. If I was in that situation, I don't know if I would have believed it either. I just hope finding the car helps in some way."

"The vehicle is being processed now. With the shape it's in, I just don't know if they'll be lucky enough to lift anything of significance from it. The license plates are missing, and the VIN number was damaged in the fire. So, I doubt we'll have the information needed to run the registration."

"This guy is pretty good at covering his tracks."

"That's been the problem all along."

"Do you want to sit down? I can fix us something to drink."

"I really should go." There was obvious hesitation in his body language. The way he stared at her just now and the intensity in his eyes sent a heatwave coursing through her. "Unless you want me to stay."

When she stood her legs trembled, and she was afraid they would buckle. She said breathlessly, "Why don't you stay."

He closed the gap between them in the space of a heartbeat and swept her into his arms. The warmth of his lips as they crushed down on her evoked the sensation of floating above the clouds. He slid his tongue inside her mouth, and he tasted just as she remembered. Deepening the kiss, he drew her into him, hand sliding down, past her hip, and cupping her behind. She moaned sweetly when his other hand followed suit.

He tore his lips away, and planted kisses down the inside of her neck, trailing them back up to her earlobe, whispering soft and low, "You're mine. And you always have been."

Heart palpitating a mile a minute, all she could do was respond, "Yes."

Finding her lips again, he backed her up against the couch. And before she knew it, he laid her down, and climbed on top of her, his hips urging her legs apart. He drove his hardness against her, and she let out another moan, wrapping her legs around his hips to feel every thrust. His fingers loosened the buttons of her blouse, and the fire raged out of control as she waited breathlessly for him to finish the job.

Where Cole was concerned, making love to him was like the first time, every time. It had always been a perfect, comfortable thing, as if slipping into a snug-fitting glove. But she hadn't experienced his touch in so long. There had been so many nights spent yearning for it, and in agony because she didn't have it. But the warmth of his lips, the touch of his hands was all over her now, branding her body, just the way they had done when she'd been a teenager under his spell.

Her shirt lay open, breasts exposed beneath his roving gaze. "You are a beautiful woman, you know that? God, I've missed you."

"What will you do now that you have me?"

He chuckled, getting up and taking her by the hand. "Let's go back to your room, and I'll show you."

The doorbell rang.

Their eyes meet. "Shh," he said, putting a finger to her lips. "Maybe they'll go away."

The sound buzzed again. Then loud knocking. "I know you're in there. Your car is in the driveway."

Jenna's gaze floated toward the ceiling. "It's Barbara."

"Just ignore her. She'll leave."

"This is Barbara Cassidy we're talking about."

"Shit." He moved away. "You better button your shirt."

More pounding on the door. "Who the hell is in there with you?"

Jenna swung open the door, and Barbara barged in. *Of course.*

Barbara stopped the minute she noticed Cole standing in the living room. Her gaze wandered over to Jenna. "Did I interrupt something?"

Cole smirked. "Would it matter?"

Now she scrutinized Jenna. "Wait a minute. Were you two…"

"No," came Jenna's quick response.

"Yes, we were," Cole said, never taking his attention off Jenna.

"Holy shit," Barbara said, face lighting up with

excitement. "Not what I expected, but this is great."

"Was great," Cole shot back.

Barbara cleared her throat. "I can leave." She headed toward the door. "As a matter of fact, I was never here."

"Barbara, wait," Jenna broke in. "You don't have to go."

"I was on my way out, anyhow," Cole said.

Barbara snorted. "It didn't look that way to me."

"Thanks for reminding me how much of a smart-ass you are. I almost forgot."

"It's called telling the truth. There's a difference."

He frowned, eyes mirroring his irritation. "Is that your definition of it?"

She strolled past him and laid her purse on the coffee table. "Look, I think it's great the two of you are bumping uglies again."

"Perhaps if you hadn't persisted on pounding on the door like a petulant child," he said, raising an eyebrow, "we might have gotten that far."

"Oh, such big words, Cole."

Jenna threw up her hands. Why was it when these two were together, she always found herself smack in the middle of their arguments?

"I'm gonna go." Cole strode toward the door.

Jenna followed. "I wish you'd stay."

He placed a kiss on her forehead. "Have a good night."

After seeing him out, she faced Barbara, shooting silent daggers at her.

"What?"

"Never mind." It's not like it would do any good to say anything anyhow.

A gigantic smile stretched across Barbara's face. "You have to tell me everything."

What were they, teenagers? "Okay," Jenna said, heading into the kitchen, "but first I'll fix us a drink."

****

The killer stood in front of his closet, stuff strewn everywhere. *Where the hell was it?* He was certain it should be in here somewhere. Just about the time he was ready to give up, he noticed the corner of the shoe box poking out from beneath a pile of clothes. The damn thing had been shoved toward the back of the highest shelf. He plucked it out, and carried it to the living room, taking a seat on the couch.

After removing the lid, he stared at the contents. When was the last time he shuffled through these keepsakes? It must have been six years. It had been easier to avoid the things inside because they reminded him of the person he used to be, and that individual died a long time ago.

There was only a handful of items in it, but the thing of interest sat right on top. He picked up the photograph and stared at the face of a young girl sitting next to Cole. What was her name? Jenny, Jennifer…no, Jenna. That was it.

The little tramp had been the one his son was so smitten with, and it had always been a mystery why. She left soon after the tragedy. Packed up and moved away with her parents, didn't she? Yes. The memory of hiding in the closet of Cole's bedroom, listening as he cried himself to sleep all those nights came back. That little bitch broke his heart, deserted him. And she was definitely the same young woman from the news segment tonight.

But why was she back again? He dropped the photo into the box and sat thinking, remembering the conversation between the two lovebirds in the restaurant that night ten years ago. It had been quite useful hiding in the shadows and listening in on them.

He'd eavesdropped many times before, and no one had been the wiser. The girl was upset over something that had happened. Nightmares, or visions, maybe some sort of spiritual phenomenon.

That's right, he suddenly recalled. The little bitch was psychic. And Cole never took it seriously.

But he did. The spiritual world was a powerful thing. Only fools ignored the divine interventions in the universe. They couldn't feel the unseen energy surrounding them. That girl tapped into it, just like him.

Realization struck, making him wonder about the precise time Jenna showed up on the scene. Could it have been when he started having complications? Was she responsible for things going wrong? Did she know about the killings?

He shot off the couch. *That was her!* She had been the one in his house that night. Something like that never happened before. Until now it had been a mystery what she was doing there, or even how such an apparition appeared out of thin air.

What could be done about it? The bitch had to be stopped. That much was clear. If he got rid of Jenna, all this bad karma would go with her. Once again, the Gods of the spiritual world offered a gift by showing this to him. He would act on it. It was time to plan an execution. His freedom depended on it.

****

Cole slogged down the hospital corridor toward

room 127, a vase of flowers in his hand. A nurse had called thirty minutes ago to let him know that Gloria Perez, the kidnap victim they rescued yesterday, was alert enough to talk. He must resemble a zombie, only having gotten about four hours of sleep last night.

The memory of the intimate moment shared with Jenna before Barbara interrupted was still there. And the cold shower this morning did not put out the fire or distract him in the least from wanting to finish what they'd started. If he could just do to her what should have been done from the moment she came back, and get it out of his system, he might be able to function again. But it was doubtful. Making love to her would only bring torture until he could do it a second time, and a third. That woman made him into a walking time bomb for God's sake.

As he approached the room, Officer Perdue sat outside the door. "Morning, Detective."

"How is everything going here?"

"Quiet. Her family and fiancé have been to visit a few times. But there's no one in there now."

Cole rapped on the door before entering. He got no response and peeked inside. She was lying in bed, watching TV. "Gloria?" he said, stepping into the room.

"Are you the detective they said was coming to talk to me?"

"Yes, ma'am. I'm Detective Rainwater, and these are for you." He set the flowers on the windowsill.

Her smile turned into a grimace of pain.

A pang of sympathy came over him. She sported two black eyes—one of them swollen shut—a cracked bottom lip, and the whole right side of her face was a mixture of black and purple. A gauze wrap covered the top of her head.

Compelled to sit beside her, he scooted the chair closer and took her hand. "I am so sorry you've suffered like this. And I promise you one thing, Gloria. I will do everything in my power to make the monster who did this to you pay."

As she lay there, straining to look at him, a tear rolled down her cheek. "You seem like a good man. And I believe you."

"I'm going to need your help though. We can get through this together."

"I know."

He couldn't help but admire her bravery and gave a warm smile.

She took a deep breath. "He's a monster. And I don't want any other women to go through what he did to me."

"How much do you remember?"

"Everything." She closed her eyes for a moment, resting against the pillow. "They told me I was drugged, and I shouldn't recall as much as I do. But I drink a couple glasses of grapefruit juice every day, done it for years. The doctor told me the juice counteracts the hypnotic effects of the drug which is most likely why I remember so much of what happened."

This was a fact—about the grapefruit juice—Cole didn't know. Figuring a person could stand to learn something new every day, he hoped this girl would provide just the break they needed.

"I was unconscious when I got to the barn," she started. "But I came to after he put the shackles on me. He raped and tortured me for so long. I thought there was no way I could survive that."

She turned her head, gazed out the window next to the bed. He'd seen this reaction often in victims as they struggled to pull themselves together. "I'm lucky to be alive," she said almost like she didn't believe it.

He squeezed her hand. "I can come back later today if you want. Give you time to rest."

She shook her head and stared at him. Determination lifting her chin. "There will be no rest for me until that animal is off the streets."

Good for her. "Can you give me a description of the guy?"

"Yes, I can."

Cole took out his pad and clicked the pen.

"He is medium height. No hair and grayish eyes. He had on camouflage gear, like a hunter, I guess. He also had a goatee."

"Is he Caucasian, black?"

"White. Maybe around sixty years old."

Jenna's description of the man she saw in her out-of-body experience came to mind. The one who sounded a lot like his deceased father. It was crazy to even entertain such a notion. Dead men do not crawl out of graves and commit murder. But something else formulated in his mind.

First, it needed to be confirmed that Gloria's attacker, and the perpetrator Jenna described, were the same guy. "Did he wear dog tags?"

Silence filled the room, and then she asked, "How did you know?"

Even though somewhere deep inside he suspected she would verify his suspicion, it was still a shock to hear it. "You happen to see the name on the tags?"

Gloria shook her head. "The only thing I remember about those things is the awful way they clinked together every time he attacked me." Tears streamed down her face, and she broke out into a sob, appearing every bit as angry as distraught.

"What are you doing?"

Cole's attention traveled to a young man standing a few feet from the door with a teddy bear in his arms. The guy rushed to Gloria's side, handing her the stuffed animal. "You're upsetting her? Who are you?"

"It's okay," Gloria said through her tears. "He's a detective and has come to ask some questions about the attack." She glanced at Cole and explained, "This is my fiancé, Greg."

Cole knew the proper thing was to introduce himself to the guy. But he didn't look receptive to niceties at the moment.

He appeared downright pissed.

"What's wrong with you? Do you think she's in any shape to answer questions? If you don't get out of here right now, I'm calling the nurse."

"Stop it!" Gloria demanded. "Sit down, Greg."

After a moment of just standing there, her fiancé reluctantly did what she asked, a scowl still present on his face.

"He hasn't come here to hurt me. He is trying to get this sicko off the streets. To do that, he must get information from me. Do you understand?"

"Yeah, but—"

"Shut it."

Inwardly Cole smiled. This girl showed courage rarely seen from victims, especially ones who had been brutalized as badly as her. Yet he could tell when enough was enough. He didn't want to push it too far.

"Thank you for being so brave," he said, squeezing her hand and then rising to his feet. "But I think I have all the information I need for today. The only thing I'd ask is if you wouldn't mind a visit from our sketch artist. With your help, he'd be able to draw a picture of what this guy looks like."

"Sure."

"You stay strong, okay?" He winked at Gloria and nodded toward her fiancé before leaving the room.

Stepping into the elevator, he reflected on the details of his father's crimes. There were twelve victims the police linked to Derek Rainwater after his suicide. A few were unsolved murders in nearby counties. Some were crimes they already knew he was responsible for, and if memory served correct, there was a missing-person's case for a body that had not been discovered until a few years ago. In all, except for the last case, the victims had been burned, the corpses disposed of in the woods. It was the same MO as the women they had been finding in this case. Their killer resembled his father, wore army fatigues, and had dog tags, just like his dad.

But the perpetrator could not be his father. The only other explanation was they had a copycat on their hands, an admirer of Derek Rainwater, someone who aspired to be just like him, even down to the man's appearance. And if the guy followed in his footsteps, Cole might find some clues in Derek's case file.

He grabbed the phone and dialed Gibbs' number. When his partner answered, he instructed him to get in contact with the sketch artist the department had used in the past and set up an appointment for the guy to meet at the hospital with the victim.

"No problem," his partner said. "Oh, and by the way, about yesterday with Jenna. I was just giving you a hard time."

"No, you weren't. But don't sweat it. You're not her type."

Gibbs chuckled. "Oh, yeah. Then who is?"

"I am."

****

Once at the precinct, Cole trekked to the evidence room where they kept old case files and found the box with his father's name on it. He took it out and carried it to his office, shutting the door behind him, as it would take time to thumb through the files, and the less disturbance, the better.

He scanned through the information, and unfortunately, there wasn't much there. Some typed documents, and a few handwritten reports. According to one of the files, no DNA had ever been recovered. The findings of the rape kits performed on the two burned victims found in the van with his father confirmed the women had been raped. As luck would have it, the burning vehicle was discovered quickly enough by a passerby and the flames extinguished in enough time as to allow the medical examiner to find vaginal tearing in the young women.

He wondered what happened to Derek's dog tags. It bothered him their suspect was also wearing a pair. Although they couldn't be the same ones, it would be a lot less worrisome if the set that belonged to his dad could be tracked down. It was a nagging intuition in the back of his mind that wouldn't let him rest, and he couldn't figure out why.

Growing up, a day did not go by that Derek didn't wear them, along with his army fatigues. When he had asked his mother about it, she'd shook her head, and explained after serving in Desert Storm, his dad had been all about the army. Derek even went so far as to keep a shaved head once returning home.

He hated this feeling, the realization of what his father had done, yet knowing how good a dad Derek had been to him. The man had never been violent. Cole couldn't come up with a single, negative memory surrounding Derek Rainwater. His dad genuinely acted as if he loved his son and wife. The monster his father had turned into with those women was not the same devoted and loving person Cole grew up with. It made no damn sense.

None of it mattered anyhow, did it? He had no care to go strolling down that what-if road again, especially now. Focusing on the task at hand was more important. Whatever it took, bringing this bastard down had become his obsession.

He noticed a signature on one of the documents. It appeared as if the detective who investigated Derek's case left his name and number. Sergeant Danny Long.

Going on a hunch, Cole picked up his phone and dialed the man's number, getting his voicemail. He ended the call without leaving a message.

Then he fired up his computer and searched for the guy. Turned out he retired from the police department a year after Derek's case. A little more digging brought up the former sergeant's address. After jotting it on a post-a-note, he left the office. If the man wouldn't answer his phone, perhaps he'd come to the door.

A fifteen-minute trip across town and he stood on

the Long's doorstep. He rang the buzzer and waited, noticing the car in the driveway. Someone was home.

An older lady with silver hair and a cheerful smile answered the door. "Can I help you?"

"Ma'am, I'm hoping to speak with Sergeant Long if he's in."

"And who are you?"

"I'm Detective Rainwater. I have a few questions about a case he worked before retiring."

She peered over her shoulder. "Danny, there's a Detective Rainwater here to see you."

It seemed like it took forever, but a short, gray-haired man finally strode to the door. "What brings you here, young man?"

"Sir, my name is—"

"I know who you are. Heard Derek's son joined the police force some years ago."

"We're investigating a case, and I believe we may be dealing with a copycat of his crimes. If you have a few minutes, I was hoping to get some information from you about your findings into my father's case."

"This have anything to do with the killings all over the news?"

"Yes."

"A copycat, huh?"

"I'm beginning to think so."

"Doesn't surprise me, with the way he's burning the bodies. Come on in, son."

Long led him into the living room. As Cole took a seat on the couch, Danny sat in the chair across from him. "You like tea?"

"We're in Texas. Who doesn't?"

Danny smiled and hollered toward the hallway.

"Dolores, can you bring two glasses of tea, please?"

Focusing his attention back on Cole, the man shook his head with incredulity. "I'm sure I'm not the first person to tell you how much you favor your dad."

"I got that a lot when I first joined the force. Now I think everyone has gotten pretty used to it."

"It was an unfair thing you had to deal with, what your father did."

"It happened a long time ago. I do my best to put it in the past and move on with my life."

"Well, it can't be easy investigating this case."

"This is my profession. I don't get emotionally involved."

"That's a commendable thing, son. So what do you want to know?"

"I didn't find any DNA evidence in Derek's file. I'm running into the same thing with this case."

"Derek Rainwater was smart. He knew how to fly under the radar. If it hadn't been for the one eyewitness who saw your father's van in the vicinity where Sara Carter, the last girl he had kidnapped, had been spotted before disappearing, we never would have suspected him. We didn't find a shred of evidence in his house linking him to the murder of any of those girls. It was the strangest thing."

Dolores carried the glasses of tea into the living room and set them down on the coffee table. Cole thanked her. She smiled and sauntered off.

"What about the findings of the rape kits?" Cole asked. "Was there evidence of a lubricant?"

"Back then, we didn't test for things like that. But if Derek had used condoms, it would have made perfect sense since he left no DNA behind. I think the fact he shaved his head made it more difficult. And he wore gloves. Forensics found a box of them outside his van."

"Did they find a pair of dog tags?"

The man just sat there with an empty expression.

"My father always wore them. Always, Sergeant Long. I've got two witnesses who have seen them around our guy's neck."

"I don't recall anything like that being rounded up from the crime scene."

"Was he wearing them when they found his body?"

"I don't believe so. You're not thinking your suspect somehow got your father's dog tags, are you?"

It was a preposterous notion. He shouldn't have even entertained it. "It's just odd. The perpetrator committing these crimes has seemed to mimic my father in so many ways."

"Can I ask you something private?"

"Sure."

"How was your dad, I mean personally?"

Cole frowned. "To be honest, he wasn't the monster at home everyone assumed he must have been. He was just a regular dad. I don't think I ever even heard him raise his voice."

"I'm not surprised to hear you say that. We talked to his friends, coworkers, and acquaintances. All of them said the same thing. There were no homicidal tendencies to speak of. Most serial killers show signs of aggression at some point in their personal lives. That was not the case with your father. He had no history of violence. It seemed to me all the pieces of the puzzle never quite fit. But we had our witness and the burned bodies of the missing teens in his van. That made it a slam dunk."

Funny he should say that, as Cole often thought the same thing. “Well, I appreciate your time, Sergeant Long. Thanks for the insight.”

The man rose from his seat the same time Cole did and walked him to the front door. They issued their goodbyes, and as he pulled off, heading in the direction of the precinct, his cell rang. Gibbs’ name came up on the screen. “What’s up?”

“Where are you?”

“On the south side of Farmersville. Why?”

“We have a dead guy. A worker for the county just reported seeing the body. A crew was out there chopping down some trees, and the employee wandered off the road into the bushes to take a leak. That’s when he saw him.”

“Where?”

“About two miles down County Road 159.”

“I can be there in five minutes.”

“I’ll see you there.”

He made a U-turn and traveled in the opposite direction.

Approaching the road, he noticed emergency vehicles right away. Cole found a place to park and hiked to the crime scene. Caution tape marked the spot where the body was. Cole flashed his badge to authorities who were blocking off the view of the body, and they stepped aside as he headed in the direction of the dead guy.

He was young. Cole guessed early twenties, wearing a light blue, long-sleeved shirt with a collar, and a pair of black trousers. He had been dressed formally for something. Perhaps an office position, or even a job interview.

He recognized the same forensic technician who had introduced him to the property owner at the last crime scene. The guy was kneeling to snap pictures of the bloody wound in the dead man's throat. Most likely caused by a knife.

"Any identification on the victim?"

He shook his head, dialing his camera in and snapping another photo. "No wallet. Nothing."

"Robbery?"

"Could be."

With the way the fellow was dressed, it didn't appear he was getting to his destination on foot. "Where's the victim's transportation?"

"Wasn't any."

Could it be a coincidence the killer they'd been tracking set his car on fire, and not a few miles down the road from where they had discovered it, there was a dead body dressed in formal clothes with no wheels? Not a chance. It was time to do some canvassing. Surely, someone around here saw this guy.

As he walked back to his car, Gibbs pulled up and rolled down the window. "Where are you off to?" his partner asked.

"I have a feeling our guy wasted this fellow back there and took off with his car. There are a few convenience stores up the road. I'm going to see if the victim stopped in any of them. Have we gotten anywhere with the list of drivers?"

Gibbs expressed frustration. "Nope."

"Why don't we broaden the search to include females? Maybe the car the perp was driving belonged to a female family member or acquaintance. If we can find the owner of the car, it will bring us closer to him."

"Sounds like a plan. The sketch artist will be meeting with Gloria Perez in about an hour or two."

"Great. I'll keep you updated on my progress out here."

Cole strolled off and climbed into the squad car. The first place to check would be the Pit Stop about a mile down the road. He knew the owner.

Lisa Duncan stood behind the cash register as he entered the store. "Good morning, Detective Rainwater."

He nodded a brief greeting. "Listen, we're trying to track down the identity of someone and—"

"Is it the dead body up the road?"

Word got around quick in a small town. "The guy was well dressed, a light, blue-collar shirt. Long sleeves and black trousers. Tall, with sandy, blond hair. Young, maybe early twenties. Did he come in here either yesterday or today?"

She chewed on her lip. "There was a young man, dressed as you said, who stopped in here yesterday morning, oh, about six thirty. He had a flat tire and purchased a can of fix-a-flat."

He glanced at the camera mounted in the corner of the ceiling, pointed at it, and said, "Have you got one of those in the parking lot?" If he could get some clear footage outside, they might be able to get a view of the vehicle the man drove. A license plate number would even be better.

"As a matter of fact, we do."

"Can I view it?"

"Hey, Charlie," she shouted toward the back of the store. "We need to see the footage from the outside camera."

A few minutes later, the kid sidled up from the center aisle. “Hey, Detective Rainwater,” he said, waving him to the back of the store. “If you’ll follow me, I’ll take you to the surveillance room.”

Once there, Cole asked the young man to cue the footage to a few minutes before Lisa told him the victim had arrived. The footage portrayed a few customers pulling up at the gas pumps, walking in and coming back out. But at about the one-and-a-half-minute mark, a silver car pulled up at the front of the store, and a man resembling the dead guy got out.

“Rewind that,” he said.

The store clerk did as he asked, and when the recording reached the point where the car was, once again, pulling into the store, Cole told the kid to freeze the frame. He leaned into the screen and noticed there was a clear shot of the vehicle’s front license plate. R17-WWK. He took the pad and pen out of the front pocket of his shirt, and wrote down the plate number, then told Charlie to play the rest of the footage.

The same man who got out of the car before, stepped around to the passenger’s side, obviously checking the front tire. Thirty seconds later, the victim wandered into the store. Cole waited for him to come back out, and when he did, there was something in his hand. He hobbled around to the flat tire, and crouched down, disappearing out of view of the camera. Soon the man’s head popped back up and he carried the item he purchased with him, throwing it into the back seat of the car before climbing in and reversing out of the parking lot. Just as Lisa said, the guy came in for a can of fix-a-flat.

Cole glanced at the kid. “I’ll need a copy of this.”

"I can have it for you in a few hours."

He laid a business card on the desk, saying, "Call me when it's ready."

Once in the car, Cole ran the license plate number through the computer. And bingo, the registered owner's name came up. Joshua Moore, at 607 Mount Pleasant Street in Sulphur Springs, Texas. A simple Internet search and he found himself staring at a picture of the dead guy, confirming they were the same. He grabbed his phone and sent a text to Gibbs, then dialed his number.

When Gibbs answered, Cole said, "Check your texts. I've sent you the license plate number of the victim's car, and his name and address."

"Wait, how the hell did you know that?"

"The victim had a flat tire at about six thirty. He bought a can of fix-a-flat at the Pit Stop. I saw the video footage of the guy pulling into the station and making the purchase. Let's put out an APB and find the bastard who stole his car."

"Damn good detective work, man."

"Compliment me after we get him into custody. Then you can buy me a beer."

"You got it."

Chapter Eight

Disbelief and anger ripped through him. The killer couldn't believe what he was seeing on the evening news. How did they find the dead guy so quickly?

It was her. Had to be. That little psychic tramp was ruining everything. Now, his plans of getting rid of her would have to be delayed. It would only be a matter of time before the police found out the identity of the poor son of a bitch he'd killed. With a little more investigation, they'd discover the man drove his car through Farmersville that morning. An APB would be put out on the vehicle, and every cop around would be looking for it—and they'd find it.

Remember, this was why you switched the plates. It would only buy a little time though. They'd figure it out, and it wouldn't take long. He needed a new set of wheels. And now, with all the heat on the street, he would have to obtain them the honest way.

It would take the entire savings he'd been socking away just in case relocating became necessary. He certainly couldn't walk into a dealership with no ID. A paper trail like that could never be risked anyhow. No, buying a car from an individual and paying for it in cash was the only way. How long would that take?

He had been lucky enough to buy the last car from his boss years ago. This time he would have to purchase one through a stranger and hope the previous owner was honest about the condition of the vehicle. There would be no time to deal with a lemon.

He picked up his phone and started searching through online classifieds. Twenty minutes later something came across his screen that might work. A blue 2006 sports utility vehicle. In great condition. Low mileage. And he had just enough money to get it. The vehicle was in the DFW area. The best thing about it, when this all blew over, he would have more room to store his victims. God, the old days of running the streets with the van were great. He reflected on memories of the time he'd picked up two little bitches on the same night, an hour apart from one another. How many serial killers had the balls to pull that off?

The contact person for the vehicle was a guy named Lucas. He dialed the number and waited for someone to pick up.

"Hello."

"I'm calling about your vehicle for sale. Is it still available?"

"Yes. I have someone interested, and they are supposed to come by tomorrow morning to look at it."

"That won't be necessary. If it's in good shape, like you say, I'll take it off your hands tonight."

"It runs great. I used it my first few years in Texas. It's been stored in the garage at my house since 2011 after I bought a new car. I was going to give it to my son when he graduated high school, but kids these days aren't interested in a 2006 model. They'd rather have a new set of wheels. You know how it is. Anyhow, I need the room in my garage, so I decided since he wouldn't want it, I'd sell it."

"I can meet you in about an hour."

"Whoa, that soon? I have an engagement this evening and—"

"I have cash."

A pause, and then, "You say an hour?"

"Maybe earlier depending on traffic."

"All right but I'm not taking less than the asking price."

"I don't expect you to."

"I'll text the address to the phone you're talking on. See you soon."

That had been less painful than imagined. He smiled and headed to the bedroom. On the floor by the bed sat a box of disguises pulled out from the other day, ready for use. Back to this again, all because of his son's ex-girlfriend. Although now he couldn't be sure how much of an ex she was. After all, it appeared Jenna was in Cole's life once more.

Soon she'd be six feet under, and his problems would go away.

He plucked out a blond wig and rummaged around for a matching mustache and sideburns. Finding a pair of glasses, he slipped them on to get a feel for them. Not too bad. They were a pair of outdated reading glasses his foster mother had given him to keep in memory of her late husband when the man passed away. Cheap bitch.

The recollection caused a disdainful snort. They'd had the nerve to think they were good parents. His foster father routinely beat the shit out of his wife. All the drunken bastard ever did was go on a rampage and run him out of the house.

He'd gotten no sympathy from the wife. Half the time she was laid up out of her mind on pills. Joining the army had been the only escape from that hellhole.

He strolled into the bathroom and glanced in the mirror while readying the wig. The face staring back was an attractive man if he did say so himself. It was a mystery where the genes came from. Good ol' Mom and Dad were strangers, and they never bothered to come looking for their kids either. Fuck all of them. He did fine on his own.

After a few minutes of work, it was amazing how his face had transformed. The reflection resembled someone out of a seventies movie. Good. Now if he added a jacket to set off the ensemble, he'd be ready to face the world.

He grabbed a bottle of cleaning solution, and a rag before heading out the door. Wiping the fingerprints off the car before ditching it was a must. Then the only thing left would be to stop by a car wash on the way to vacuum out any loose hair and clothing fibers. He'd pick a good spot close to where the purchase was going to take place and get rid of the car. Then making the rest of the trip on foot should be easy. After returning home, he would finish the business there had been no time to start. He'd scour the Internet. Find out as much about Jenna Langley as possible. This should give him enough information to plan her murder. With her out of the way, life would get back to normal. And in a month, he'd be right back to killing again.

****

Surprise lit Cole's face when he discovered a hit came in for the dead man's car. A police officer spotted the silver Camry with matching plates at the Sunrise Apartment complex in Farmersville.

"We got him now," Gibbs said, walking with Cole

through the exit doors of the precinct.

"Let's hope." But with the feeling in his gut, he wasn't so sure. It seemed a little too easy their killer had been right under their nose all this time. How smart would it be for the guy to live at an apartment with people witnessing his movements? Serial killers sought solitude, freedom to commit their crimes with no one around to see. Yet it was a big lead, and it certainly needed to be followed up on.

Cole hit the unlock button as he and Gibbs headed toward his truck. The police cruiser would not be used. They didn't want to tip off the suspect.

When they arrived, Cole pulled into a parking lot across the street where the view to the apartment was good, and they could stay out of sight. The stolen car of the dead guy was within eyeshot. Johnston and Prebis—two plainclothes detectives—were parked in a secluded spot on the opposite side of the dumpster. They faced the road. He swung in beside them and rolled down the window. "Any movement yet?" he asked Prebis, who was sitting in the driver's seat.

"Not yet."

"How long have you guys been here?"

"About ten minutes."

Cole checked his watch. It was seven ten p.m. There'd be no telling when the suspect came out of the apartment. They could be here all night. Just how he wanted to end the evening.

As he studied two kids on bicycles pedal into the complex, Gibbs broke the silence. "There's about ten females on the updated list of drivers."

"How many have we made contact with?"

"Only a handful. Channing's handling it. He's

spent most of the day tracking down the ones he could."

He didn't put much faith into that investigation. But no leaf needed to be left unturned. He'd seen too many times the simplest of leads turning out to be the one that broke the case wide open. They certainly didn't have much more to go on at this point.

"So, now that we have some time to kill, are you gonna give me a little history on you and Jenna?"

"Why?" He stared at him suspiciously.

"Man, it's not like that. The other day at the precinct, I got the message. You two have a thing. I've been your partner for how long? I don't know shit about your personal life, yet you seem to know everything about mine."

"That's because there's not much to tell."

"Bullshit. A beautiful woman like that."

She was about the only thing worthwhile that ever happened to him. "We met when we were fifteen. Dated for two years in high school."

"That woman doesn't look like a high school girl. What happened between you two?"

"Her parents found out about my father, and they kept us away from one another."

"And now, all of a sudden, she's come back into your life?"

"Yeah. Something like that."

"You don't want to talk about this, do you?"

"No."

"I don't get it. If a hot-ass woman like that showed interest in me, I'd tell anyone who'd listen."

Believe me, I haven't gotten that woman out of my head in ten years.

"Does she know how you feel about her?"

He stared at his partner. "How do *you* know how I feel about her?"

"Um, because you've been an irritable bastard ever since she's come into the picture. You can lie to Jenna, but we don't lie to each other. Know what I mean?"

He chuckled. "It's that obvious, huh?"

"Yeah, man. So, tell me you have a plan."

He sighed, gripping the steering wheel. "I'm sure she's going back to Georgia as soon as her business deal is finished."

"And you're going to let that happen?"

"It's not as if I can stop it." Cole would like nothing more. But if she stayed, it must be her decision. Jenna had left once, and this time it would have to be clear she was here because she couldn't live without him. There couldn't be any doubt she wanted the relationship just as much as he did.

Silence filled the truck as he caught a glimpse of someone plodding down the breezeway of the apartment and taking the stairs to the ground level. A skinny, young man with shoulder-length, dark hair made his way across the parking lot, approaching the car they had been staking out. He tugged something from his pocket and aimed it straight ahead. The vehicle beeped, and the headlights flashed.

Cole glanced at Prebis and nodded. They both turned over their ignitions.

By the time they made it to the apartments, the guy was about to climb into the driver's seat. They pulled in quickly, surrounding him. Cole and Gibbs jumped from the truck, the other two detectives fast on their heels.

The young man glanced over his shoulder, straightened, and dropped the Styrofoam cup as they rushed toward him. Cole got there first, throwing the guy up against the hood, frisking, and then slapping the handcuffs on.

"What…who…what are you…d…doing?"

"You're under arrest."

"For what?"

"The car you're driving is stolen. And the guy who owned it is dead. What do you know about that?"

"What? N…nothing. This is my car."

Cole thrust him toward Prebis' unmarked car, and Gibbs held open the door while he settled the young man into the back seat.

As he swung the door shut, the guy's irate shouting penetrated through the window. "Who are you, people? I didn't kill anybody! I'm going to be late for work!"

Cole climbed in the truck and waited for Gibbs. Once his partner shut the door, he gazed at him and said, "You expect me to believe that skinny, pimple-faced kid is responsible for three killings and two kidnappings. He looks like he'd shit his pants if I hollered boo."

"Then what's he doing with a dead man's car?"

"I don't know. But he didn't kill him to get it."

****

After pulling up to his house and climbing out of the sports utility vehicle, the killer peered back at the new ride and grinned. Lucas had been telling the truth after all. The vehicle was in great condition, fewer than twenty thousand miles, new tires, and not a scratch on it. It would be a wonderful tool for kidnapping. But before it could be utilized for that purpose there was a pressing nuisance, by the name of Jenna Langley, that needed to be dealt with. The whole trip home he had been looking forward to planning the bitch's murder. The first order of business would be figuring out how to track her down.

He whistled cheerfully striding through the front door, grabbed a beer from the fridge, and settled in on the sofa for some enlightening exploration. He slid the phone out of his jacket pocket and punched Jenna's name into the Google search bar.

The first result that came up was an article from a business magazine listing her name in the description. He clicked on it, and after reading a few paragraphs, learned that Jenna had sold a successful janitorial company a few years ago in Georgia and was now specializing in business consulting. Quite the little busybody, huh?

Then he ran across a link for her social media page. The profile picture depicted a carefree woman clad in a flowery summer dress standing on a beach. Judging by the green color of the ocean behind her, it was a good guess the photo had been taken somewhere in Florida. The background awakened memories of the fishing trips he used to take with one of his army buddies in Pensacola not long after his military discharge.

His heart rate picked up as he scrolled through her posts and ran across one of the more recent ones. *I'm off to Texas tomorrow morning for my first business consultant gig at R&H Janitorial Services. Wish me luck.*

Out of all the comments of encouragement, one stood out from a Robert Langley. *I just know you're going to do great, sweetheart.* Jenna's father left a cute heart emoji in his reply.

The killer grinned derisively. How darling. But the

remark from her mother, Amanda Langley, wasn't so inspiring. *I just can't imagine how you can consider going to Texas again. But you've always done what you wanted, haven't you?*

No words of praise from that cold bitch. He had to agree though. Jenna thought she was smarter than everyone else. But he was about to beat her at her own game.

The killer clicked off her social media page, and typed R&H Janitorial Services into the search bar. Bingo. The owner's name was Stanley Benton. Hours of operation were eight a.m. to six p.m. The place was located at south McDonald Street in McKinney. Awareness came over him. He'd passed by the establishment dozens of times. A mental picture of the place developed in his mind. It was situated between the bank and the hardware store. If the guy hired Jenna as a business consultant, the expectation she'd be there most of the day would be likely. He'd arrive early in the morning and perform a little surveillance. Wait for the stupid bitch to show up. And when she left…

Jenna Langley would be a sitting duck. The pursuit was going to be as easy as hunting a trapped animal. She'd never know he had her in his sights. The killer strolled into the kitchen for another beer. This was worth celebrating.

****

Cole sat in the interrogation room across from the young man they'd taken into custody. "What's your name?"

With an irritated expression, the guy averted his gaze. "Zack Sexton. What the hell is this all about?"

"Where were you yesterday morning between the

hours of six and eight?" he asked, going with the time of death the coroner had given them for the latest victim.

"I was at Lucky Seven, the gas station off Highway 78 where I work."

"What time did you leave?"

"Eight o'clock. Are you going to answer my question?"

"I'm not here to answer your questions. You're here to answer mine."

"This is bullshit."

"Where did you get the car?"

"My car?"

"That's not your car. It belonged to a guy we found dead this morning. Care to explain that?"

"It's my car. And I didn't kill anybody."

"I didn't say anything about you killing somebody. Did you murder someone, Zack?"

"No!"

"Then who did? You have his car. Just tell the truth. We're not going to let this go."

"Why are you saying my car belongs to some dead guy?"

"Because the license plates came back as a match. It's the same make and model."

Zack stood now, shock and anger prominent on his expression. "That's impossible. I bought that car two years ago from the car dealership off Highway 5 in McKinney. It was a used car."

"You can verify this?"

"Yes. I'm still making the payments."

Cole grabbed a pen and took possession of the pad. "Who do I call to check that information?"

"Yellow Tree Financial. The car is under my mom's name, Ebony Sexton. Now can I go? If I don't get to work, they're going to fire me."

"Hang tight, Zack," Cole said, rising to his feet and crossing the room. "I'll make sure your employer knows you're being delayed."

As soon as Cole closed the door, both Channing and Gibbs were waiting just outside for him. He shoved the pad against Gibbs' chest. "Call Yellow Tree Financial. See if they'll verify payments are being made on the car." Then he strode down the hall.

Gibbs hollered after him, "Where the hell are you going, man?"

"I'm going to Lucky Seven to check on his alibi. That kid in there is not your killer."

"What do you want us to do with him?" Channing asked.

"Hold him until I get back."

He sauntered out the door, got in the police cruiser, and headed for the gas station.

An older lady manned the cash register when Cole strolled in, a hint of annoyance on her face. He flashed his badge. "I'm Detective Rainwater with the Farmersville PD. Zack Sexton is running late due to a police matter."

Her mouth dropped open. "I was wondering where he was. Did he get in trouble with the law?"

"No, ma'am. Can you tell me what time he arrived for work yesterday?"

"He was here at eight. Why?"

"Who was working with him?"

"I had to pull a double yesterday. We are short-staffed. I was here for half of his shift."

"Who came in after that?"

"Jamie. I believe she clocked out some time in the afternoon."

"Do you have her number?"

She appeared skeptical. "We're not supposed to give that information out."

"I'm a detective. It's okay."

She took out her phone and searched the contacts. "Here it is," she said, holding the device out.

Cole punched the digits into his phone and waited for someone to answer.

"Hello."

"Jamie?"

"Yes."

"My name is Cole Rainwater. I'm a detective with the Farmersville PD. Can you tell me what hours you worked yesterday, at Lucky Seven?"

A pause and then, "Is everything all right?"

"Everything is fine. I just need you to answer the question."

A customer shuffled over to the counter, and Cole stepped aside so the cashier could ring up his purchases. Jamie answered, "I got there at one a.m., and left at ten a.m."

"Was Zack present the whole time?"

"No. He left at about eight in the morning, when his shift ended."

"Okay, thank you."

Cole waited for the customers to walk away, and as a few more wandered in, he asked, pointing toward the camera, "I see you have a camera in here. What about outside?" He had a hunch, and it would be interesting to see how it panned out.

The woman nodded, lost in thought. "I'm pretty sure there's one out there."

"What needs to be done for me to access the footage?"

She was stunned for a minute, and then, "I can help you with that."

"Great."

"Just a minute." She headed toward the back of the store. A few minutes later, she marched up with someone on her heels. "Mike can take care of the customers while I show you to the office."

He followed her to a small room, and she led him to the security screens. "What time period would you like to see?"

"Go ahead and cue up yesterday, about six thirty in the morning."

As the footage played, and Cole noticed nothing of significance, he had her speed it up a bit, until the same type of car the dead man drove came into view. "Slow it down for me, please."

When she did, he saw the license plate plain as day. It was a match to the dead guy's. The car rolled out of sight toward the north side of the parking lot. There was nothing for a good five minutes. And then the vehicle returned—this time cutting across the parking lot, and stopping in front of the main road, waiting for a traffic break.

"Pause it." He asked her to blow up the screen but this time he could not get a clear view of the plate.

"Can you rewind it to the point where the car originally pulls into the lot?"

"Sure."

The second time, he noticed the rust spot on the

driver's side door. Zack's car did not have that. *I'll be damned. The son of a bitch switched out the plates.*

He walked out of the store in disbelief. His hunch was right.

After climbing into the car, he called Gibbs. "Hey, man, our guy was here and switched out the plates with Zack's car. And it happens to be the same make and model. What are the chances?"

"How do you know?"

"I saw it on video. Here at the store."

"Did you get a positive ID on the perp?"

"No. I didn't see him get out of the car, but the one he drove into the parking lot has a rust stain on the door. The kid's car doesn't. I noticed the victim's license plate on the vehicle when he pulled in."

"Holy shit. Oh, and we finally have the sketch from the kidnap victim. Doesn't resemble Zack at all."

"Take a picture and send it to my phone."

"All right. So, I guess we're releasing the kid then."

"Yep. Might want to tell him to order another set of plates though."

Chapter Nine

Two days had passed since Jenna last spoke to Cole. He didn't sound optimistic about the progress of the case during their last phone call. When telling her about the latest discoveries, she'd detected a strong hint of exhaustion in his voice. This investigation was getting to him in the worst way. She wanted to help but had no idea how. Jenna hadn't had any more psychic episodes since the vision of the burning car.

It had been good to hear his voice. And honestly, it was the whole reason she called. Since the intimacy they shared, thoughts of Cole dominated her mind. But he did not mention anything about their time together while on the phone. Why was he avoiding the subject?

None of it mattered. Once the truth came out, he wouldn't want anything more to do with her. But that didn't stop Jenna from wishing things could be different. Her secret would eventually come out and facing it couldn't be avoided much longer. When they were together a few nights ago, it had been as if they'd never been apart. It wasn't realistic though. They'd been wrenched away from each other a long time ago, and her confession would only ensure things stayed that way. No matter what happened, the time had come to level with Cole. She couldn't live with the thought of deceiving him any longer.

She took the elevator down to the parking garage.

The doors opened. No one was around, and the silence sent fear crawling up her spine. *What's wrong with you*? The visions had stopped over the last few days, and she'd been more at ease now since arriving in Texas. It had been nice to experience normalcy again. But now her intuition warned her something was off.

Don't be an idiot. Everything is fine. She calmed down by remembering the professor's words. *He can't see you.*

So why the hell did it feel as if eyes were on her?

She took a deep breath and continued marching toward the car, picking up the pace. Jenna clicked the unlock button, and the vehicle beeped, startling her. She was so on edge the sound of her breathing intensified. She peered over her shoulder. No one was there.

She finally arrived at her car and relief washed over her. She crawled in quickly, hitting the lock button, and adjusting the mirror to view the back seat. It was empty. *What were you expecting, the boogeyman?*

Turning over the ignition, the engine purred, helping with relaxation. She needed to calm down. No one crouched in the shadows waiting to attack her. It had been a long week. Allowing her imagination to run wild like this was foolish.

Pulling out of the parking garage, she convinced herself nothing was out of the ordinary. She drove down the ramp and the night sky opened, the full moon casting a soft glow across the parking lot. *You see, it's all good.* She turned on the radio, which helped to relieve this awful anxiety, and hummed along with the music. A sign alerted her to the highway ramp ahead.

Time passed quickly, and before long, she was on the curvy stretch of road that led to the rental house.

Even though she'd managed to quiet her nerves, now and then, a glance in the rearview mirror helped to keep them that way. No one was following behind, and her paranoia ebbed away.

Jenna finally pulled into the driveway and killed the engine. As she walked through the door, panic rose again due to the darkness of the house. She flipped on the living room light first thing and locked the door behind her, then trekked through the house turning on lights and checking doors and windows. Although everything appeared as it had been upon leaving the house, she couldn't seem to shake the apprehension that something was terribly wrong.

The phone rang, and she jumped again. *You must stop this.* Emily's name popped up on the screen. Relief washed over her. "Hey, you," she said, eyes closing and breathing a heavy sigh.

"Hi, Momma. Whatcha' doing?"

"Oh, just getting home. How about you, kiddo?"

"I have a surprise for you."

"Oh, yeah?"

"Me, Grandma, and Grandpa are coming to Texas to see you."

"What? You have school."

"Silly, Momma. Spring break starts tomorrow. And it's my birthday too, remember?"

"Of course, I remember."

As much as she missed her daughter and wanted to see the child, with everything going on, now was not the time. But trying to persuade Emily not to come would break the girl's heart. She would never forgive her. Instead, Jenna said, "How in the world did you talk your grandparents into that?"

"They forgot my birthday last year and—"

"They promised you could have anything you wanted for your birthday this time."

"Yep."

"You are a sly little girl, know that?"

She giggled. "I can't wait to see you."

"Me too, honey. Oh, how I have missed you."

"Can you get off work for my birthday tomorrow?"

"I suppose I can arrange that."

"What will we do?"

"Well, I don't know. We can go to the zoo and maybe the aquarium. How does that sound?"

Emily squealed. "It'll be so much fun, Momma."

"What time shall I pick you up from the airport?"

"Grandma said at eleven o'clock tomorrow."

"It's a date then."

Amanda's voice carried over the phone.

The child sighed. "I gotta go. Grandma says it's time for bed."

"Don't forget to brush your teeth and say your prayers."

"Yes, ma'am."

"I love you. Sleep tight."

"Love you too, Momma."

Although Jenna was excited at the prospect of seeing her daughter again, she was leery about Emily coming to Texas with a killer running loose. And her arrival caused another complication. She would have to come clean with Cole before the girl got here. Emily could not be put in the middle of that drama.

After searching the phone's contacts for Cole's number, she just stared at it, unable to decide what to do. With Emily's flight time, her window of opportunity was limited. He would either need to be told tonight or first thing tomorrow morning.

She carried the phone to the bedroom and set it on the dresser, deciding against making the call tonight. There would be time to do it in the morning, before heading out to the airport. *It isn't like you to push things to the last second.* But this was different. It would be one of the hardest things she'd had ever had to do and doing it over the phone would be difficult enough.

As soon as she opened the drawer to get her nightclothes, a vision came over her. She slumped to the floor. Glass shattered somewhere in the distance, and a man's gloved hand breached the gaping hole of the French door pane, disengaging the bolt. The door swung open, hinges creaked, and the killer stepped inside, dressed in black. He carefully made his way into the living room.

He crept around to the kitchen with a knife clutched in his hand. Jenna's breath caught the moment she realized the room he peered into was the same as the one belonging to the rental house.

Oh my God, is he in here?

Fear rained down on her. As much as she struggled to move, nothing happened, and it was a horrifying reality knowing until this vision played out, she would essentially be paralyzed.

He's going to kill me right here while I'm helpless, and I can't do anything about it. Please, somebody, help me!

He turned into the hallway. Now approached the guest bedroom. The killer stopped and peeked inside, then skulked past the bathroom, moving to her bedroom at the end of the hall.

In another minute he would be at her door.

She fought tirelessly to move.

Then miraculously, Jenna's arm twitched, knees slowly bent, and she clutched the top of the dresser. Vision blurred, she struggled to her feet just as her door creaked open. Her knees wobbled, but she couldn't give in to the weakness. She must go now. If she faltered, he'd have her in his grasp.

She managed to make it to the door, fumbling with the lock.

Just as it opened, the sound of his scream thundered through her. "Where do you think you're going, you little bitch?"

On shaking legs she stumbled to the patio, across the stepping-stones, and toward the iron gate leading out of the backyard. She no sooner flung open the gate and ran across the front yard, gaining momentum, that his voice boomed out again. And it was so close.

"You're dead. Do you hear me? I'm going to fucking kill you!"

The neighbor's house came into view, and Jenna headed straight for it in a blind panic. She ran up the front steps and banged on the door. "Open the door! Please help me!"

She continued to pound on it. Then the horrifying possibility they may not have been home hit her. The killer would be coming around the corner any second now, and there was no way in hell she would have time to make it to the next house before he caught her.

She held down the buzzer. "Open the door!"

He grabbed her from behind, dragging her off the porch.

Jenna cried out, kicking and flailing.

The porch light came on.

He released her, and she fell to the ground.

The door swung open. A brown-haired man stood in the light of the doorway in his boxer shorts. "Are you okay, miss?"

She staggered to her feet, breathing a sigh of relief with tears streaming down her face. "Somebody broke into my house and tried to attack me."

"Dear Lord," the man said, opening the door wider so she could enter.

"I just need to use your phone to call the police."

"Are you sure you're all right?"

She nodded, heart beating a mile a minute, body trembling so severely she was struck with a sudden fear that her legs would buckle.

The man helped Jenna into the house and showed her to the kitchen, drawing out a chair. "Why don't you sit down, and I'll go get the phone for you."

She fell into it, gasping. "Thank you so much."

As soon as the neighbor returned, handing the phone to Jenna, she took it and dialed Cole's number, surprised she remembered it in her state. He picked up after the third ring. The words came out of her mouth of their own accord. "He broke into my house. He kept screaming he was going to kill me."

"Who?"

"The man from my visions."

"Where are you?"

"I'm at the neighbor's house. I managed to get away. But he almost had me, Cole. Jesus Christ, he must have followed me home or was there waiting."

"Are you okay? Are you hurt?"

"No." All at once the dam burst, and she couldn't

control the sobbing that came over her. "Can you come to my house, please? I'm afraid he'll come back."

"It's okay, sweetheart. Just calm down. I won't let that happen. I'm leaving now. Whatever you do, stay where you are until I get there."

"I'm not going anywhere." She clicked the end button on the phone and laid it on the table, shell shocked. How did he know where to find her and who she was? He had to have recognized her from the spirit walk and somehow tracked her down.

She'd come so close to becoming the next face in the morning paper.

****

Cole cursed the slow traffic as he made his way to Jenna's place. It was a twenty-minute drive to her rented house, and he was certain she must be scared to death. How the hell did the son of a bitch find her? And had it been a coincidence he'd chosen this victim? No, it had been done intentionally, that much Cole was sure of. But what would be the point of murdering her?

Did the assailant know him? It wasn't a secret Cole was the son of a notorious serial killer, the same murderer this guy seemed to be obsessed with. Did he go after Jenna to get to him? And how did the bastard know she had been a part of his past? Things just took a personal turn with this guy. And he would have to figure out the connection. Beefing up security wasn't a question at this point. Jenna would need to be watched around the clock. Who better to take care of her than him? He'd see to her safety, and risk his life doing it if necessary. This animal would not get near Jenna again.

Finally, he pulled into the neighbor's driveway. Cole had already gotten word to Gibbs, so a team was on the way to Jenna's place.

She raced out of the house as soon as he opened the truck door. She approached, appearing beyond distraught. He climbed out, heart beating wildly. The minute they were face to face Jenna fell into his arms. Believing her from the beginning might have prevented the attack. This was his fault. If he'd only listened.

Cole held her tightly while she sobbed against his chest. "I'm so sorry, honey. It's going to be okay," he promised.

"How did he find me?"

"Listen to me." He gently lifted her chin, so their eyes met. "We are going to figure this out. I will not let him hurt you. From this moment on, I'll keep you safe. I promise on my life."

When her head slumped, he tipped her chin, forcing her to meet his gaze. "Do you trust me?'

After a moment, she nodded. "Yes. I trust you."

"C'mon then," he said, heading in the direction of the rental house, a protective arm around her waist. "I think the guys are at your place."

Three squad cars were parked in her driveway. The team of investigators had arrived. Before stepping foot inside, Cole draped his windbreaker around her shoulders, and urged her toward one of the chairs on the front porch. "I need you to stay out here while we check things inside."

She stopped dead and struggled against him. "No. Don't leave me alone."

The fear reflected in her eyes made it clear she would not be persuaded. He sighed. "Okay. But you must stay close to me. We can't contaminate the crime scene."

She nodded.

They made their way down the hall. Gibbs stood at the end, his back to them. The master bedroom door was open, and his partner leaned against the doorframe, just before the threshold.

Gibbs turned around when he must have heard them approaching, and said, “Watch your step. I think we have a decent set of shoe impressions here.”

Cole inched a little closer and glanced down. Sunk into the plush carpet was the distinct shape of a set of sneakers a few feet inside the door. Judging from the depth of them, the perp must have stood in this spot watching his victim. Anger coursed through him. How long did the sick bastard stalk her before she realized he had been in the same room? Christ.

Jenna spoke up. “He was toying with me. Standing right here while I struggled to get off the floor.”

“What do you mean?” Cole asked.

“When he broke in through the front door, I saw him doing it. I was over there,” she said, pointing toward the dresser, “getting my nightclothes when I was struck with the vision. It made me weak like it always does, and I sank to the floor. I heard the bedroom door open, and I fought to get to my feet. And he was watching me for God’s sake.”

“Wait,” Gibbs broke in. “Visions?”

Ignoring him, Cole asked her, “How did you get away?”

A mystified look came over her face; she shook her head. “I guess when I finally got control of my functions, I moved quicker than I thought. But he was so close behind me the whole time. I managed to unlock the door and run out the back, all the way to the neighbor's house. I pounded on the door but got no answer. Then, he tackled me from behind and tried to drag me away. After the neighbor finally opened the door, the guy dropped me and ran."

A chill slid down Cole's spine. Jesus, if it hadn't been for the neighbor coming to the door at the last minute. He put his arm around Jenna and held her close, thanking God she'd managed to get away. There was no denying now how much she still meant to him. Losing her again would be unthinkable.

"Let's get the Stati-Lifts for these shoe prints," he told Gibbs. "Anything else so far?"

"Not yet. We need to dust the door where he entered."

"Doubt you'll find anything. He's wearing gloves."

Jenna added, "Yes. I've seen him with them on."

Gibbs appeared confused. "You've seen him?"

"Never mind," Cole said. "It's a long story. I'm taking Jenna to my place until this blows over. Call the precinct and arrange for an officer escort to be with her at all times when I can't be."

"Why did he come after her, Cole?" Gibbs wanted to know, appearing intent on getting an answer.

"I can't be sure. But I think it has something to do with me."

"Explain."

"Right now, I have to get Jenna settled."

"Listen, if you know something you're not telling me, I—"

"It's late. We can talk tomorrow. What are the chances of grabbing some clothes out of here for her?"

Gibbs just stared at him.

"Never mind. I'll come back tomorrow."

He glanced at Jenna. “Where is your purse?”

She pointed down the hall. “I left it in the kitchen.”

“Okay, let’s go.”

“I’ll follow you in my car.”

“No way. I’m not taking any chances. You can ride with me.”

“I have to work, Cole. I can’t leave my car here.”

“I’ll have someone drop it by my place in the morning.”

She nodded and they headed down the hall.

****

He should have hightailed it out of there the moment Jenna’s neighbor opened the door and saved the little slut. Instead, the killer now crouched behind shrubs as authorities inspected every inch of the yard. The front door stood open. He picked up his binoculars, identifying broken pieces of glass just beyond the threshold where he had busted out the bottom pane earlier to unlock the deadbolt and get to her.

Flashing lights from roof bars on the squad cars cast a blue, red, and white reflection across the bricks of the rental house, bringing back the memory of the time they had sent the cavalry to his house to drag him away to the looney bin many years ago. He should have reenlisted in the army where killing was acceptable, even expected. But it wasn’t the kind of bloodshed that quelled the hunger of the beast inside. No, taking things to the ultimate level had been the only alternative.

But he screwed up again. It should have been apparent since the psychic bitch had seen many of the other murders he’d committed, she’d see her own. This new awareness posed a serious obstacle.

How did someone kill a person who saw their

murder before it happened?

"Dammit."

She had been right there, within grasp, and the opportunity to eliminate the threat slipped away because of careless stupidity. Instead of standing there watching Jenna struggle to get to her feet, the wise thing to do would have been to apprehend the target before she got away. But watching her fight to get her mobility back had been far too entertaining to resist. He never expected she'd move so quickly once it happened.

Jenna Langley had been a hair's breadth away.

Now there might as well be a continent between them. From the appearance of things, the police were all over this close encounter like fruit flies on a rotting banana. How could he get to her now?

Scanning the area with the binoculars, the killer caught a glimpse of two figures moving across the yard. As they stepped onto the porch under the glow of light, it became obvious the silhouettes were Jenna and Cole. She had an oversized jacket draped over her shoulders, and they were heading in the direction of the table and chairs.

But at the last minute, Jenna scurried away, rushing toward the door. She appeared distraught and fearful. Cole approached her in an instant, and the two exchanged words. They peered over at the table and Jenna shook her head with an air of refusal. Finally, Cole slipped his arm around her waist, and they stepped through the doorway together.

The little bitch was too afraid to sit outside unaccompanied. He doubted another opportunity to get her alone would present itself. Approaching the next step from a completely different angle was necessary. Although the planning would be a challenge, thinking outside the box had been his specialty. He needed some way to lure her to him using nonviolent tactics, or he'd risk Jenna tapping into her psychic abilities again.

Ten minutes later, the couple walked outside and headed straight for Cole's pickup truck. As they climbed into the cab and the motor roared to life, it dawned on him Cole was taking Jenna to his house. No doubt, from now on the bitch would have a police escort with her, making the strategy of getting her alone that much harder to attain. But nothing worthwhile ever came easy, did it? This was far from over, and he'd have to step up his game. His saving grace to this predicament existed. It was out there somewhere. He just needed to stumble across it.

Chapter Ten

As he drove them toward his house, Cole spared Jenna a glance to check on her. She stared straight ahead, one hand in her lap, the other on the seat, fingers splayed. He slid his hand over hers. "I won't let that bastard get near you," he promised. "I'll keep you safe."

For a minute she said nothing, then, "What did you mean back there—when you said his coming after me had something to do with you?"

He let out the breath he'd been holding. "I'm sure we're dealing with a copycat of my father. This guy seems to know a lot about him. And I believe he knows about me, too. I can't figure out how he connected you to me, but somehow he did. I think he's made it personal against me by going after you."

"How did he know who I am or where to find me?"

Shaking his head, Cole said, "I don't know, but you better bet your ass I'm going to find out."

They hung a right on Main Street, and Jenna said, "We have another problem."

"What?"

"It's my daughter, Emily. She and my parents are catching a flight here tomorrow. She talked them into coming for spring break."

Emily. Now he had a name for the child she shared with another man. Jealousy riffled a path up his spine—

totally unjustified of course.

It wasn't as if he'd remained celibate after she took herself out of the picture. But none of those relationships were serious enough to include children. Hell, none lasted much more than a month or two. Jenna's leaving ruined him. He no longer had a heart to give to someone else. She'd packed up and took it with her to Georgia.

Thoughts of dealing with Amanda Langley made things worse. After finding out how she had kept them apart, Cole didn't know if he could stand to look at the woman. He withdrew his hand. "Call them back and tell them they can't come right now."

"How am I supposed to do that?"

"You'll have to figure it out. With everything going on, it's not a good idea."

"I know, but I can't."

"Can't what?" he said, flashing a look of annoyance at her.

"Tell them not to come."

"You don't have a choice."

"I'm not going to break my daughter's heart. Emily is looking forward to this and would never understand."

After pulling into his driveway, he killed the engine before turning to her in the deafening silence. "What's worse, putting your daughter in the middle of this, or upsetting her?"

She sat quiet for a moment. "Trust me. I have considered it. The flight is already booked. I don't have the heart to—"

"Where would they stay? At your place, where you were almost kidnapped?"

"I was hoping…"

The light dawned. “No way. They can’t stay here.” He jerked a thumb at the windshield. “What you’re looking at is a small, two-bedroom house. We’d crawl all over each other.”

She faced the windshield, chin stiff. “I’ll rent them a room somewhere else then.”

He couldn’t believe her failure to see reason. “You are in protective custody right now. What do you expect—”

“You don’t understand.” She faced him. “Believe me, it’s not as simple as you think.”

He searched her eyes and could see this was a real concern. “What do you want me to do?”

“Help me figure this out.”

He sighed. This woman would be the death of him. “I just don’t think it’s a good idea.”

“Neither do I. But they are coming.”

Dammit. “Okay. Give me time to think about it. We’ll work something out. I can always find a jail cell for your mother.”

She elbowed him, laughing.

It was good to see Jenna’s spirits lift in the face of all this. “What? She’d be safe.”

“Stop.”

“Okay, okay. We won’t throw her behind bars.”

“Well, if you must.”

They both exited the truck. After approaching the porch, she grabbed him by the arm, turning him to face her. “I just wanted to say thank you.”

“For what?”

“Being here for me.”

The raw emotion in her eyes caused something to snap in him, and he drew Jenna close, leaned in slowly, and captured her lips. As the kiss deepened, Cole realized after tonight nothing would be the same between them. He was forever lost in the extraordinary warmth of this woman, the softness of her mouth as she moved with him in perfect motion.

His lips traveled down to the sweet nectar of her throat, getting lost in the lilac scent of auburn hair. He breathed her in, heart beating wildly. Cole had wanted so long to have his teenage sweetheart this way again, pliant in his arms, willing to the needs that had been burning within him since the day she'd left.

She belonged to him now. And tonight, he would take his time drinking her up. He nibbled her ear and whispered hoarsely. "Let's go inside."

With bated breath, he unlocked the door, and stepped inside, his hand on the small of her back. Cole swung the door shut, and she stood there close to the wall, moonlight from the window setting her skin aglow. He couldn't resist and stepped toward his only weakness.

Gently pinning her against the wall, his lips started at Jenna's mouth, working their way down to her chin, gliding across her throat, winding toward the woman's cleavage. Every rise and fall of her chest reverberated through him. His fingers worked the buttons of her blouse.

Her hand steadied his. "I have to use the bathroom."

He chuckled. "This isn't going to end the same way it did that time we rented a motel room in Dallas and you were too afraid to come out of the john, is it?"

She laughed. "You remember that?"

"How could I forget. The cold shower didn't help. I

suffered all night."

"I did that to you, didn't I?"

He leaned into her. "Yes, you did. And it was awful."

"Well, I was a virgin," she whispered back.

"I know. I eventually fixed that problem for you. It took me a whole week, but…"

"Where's your bathroom, Casanova?"

He stepped away and pointed down the hall. "Second door to the left."

She maneuvered around him, laid her purse on the coffee table, and ambled away.

He took a deep breath, unbuckled his holster, and carried it over to the table. Just then a phone rang. Cole plucked his cell from the holder and realized that wasn't where the noise was coming from. It rang again, and something lit up in the side pouch of Jenna's purse. He grabbed the phone, and a nagging voice told him this was crossing the line to intruding on her privacy. Cole didn't know what excuse could be used for digging it out of her purse, but he'd think of one later. He had to know who was calling Jenna this late.

The name, Emily, popped up on her screen. He answered. "Hello."

"Who is this?"

The voice of a child told him it must be her daughter. "Cole. I'm a friend of your mother."

"Oh. She told me about you."

He frowned. "Oh yeah?"

"Momma said she knew you from when she lived in Texas."

"That's right. I'm an old friend."

"Me, Grandma, and Grandpa are coming there

tomorrow. I'll get to meet you."

He smiled, unconsciously getting wrapped up in the conversation with her. The girl sounded like a sweet kid. "Yes, you will."

"It's my birthday tomorrow. Did you know?"

"No. I didn't. How old will you be?"

"Nine."

An outrageous thought took a slow turn around his brain. "Is that right? And you were born March 7th, huh?"

"Yep. Momma wouldn't want me calling this late. I'm supposed to be asleep. But I forgot to tell her the gate number for the airport. Can you tell her it's gate nineteen?"

"Sure. I'll tell her."

"Okay. Good night, Cole."

"Good night, Emily."

Cole slumped against the couch, hardly processing the shock. He knew exactly what month Jenna left town. Unless she'd been sleeping with someone else during the time they were together…

She strolled into the room, and he dropped the phone on the table. "That was Emily," he said, eyes heated and piercing. "She called to tell you to pick her up at gate nineteen."

She stood there speechless. In her expression, the fact he figured out the truth was apparent.

"When were you going to tell me I have a child?"

Swallowing visibly, Jenna lowered her head. "Tonight."

He shot off the couch. "You wait until the night before she arrived to tell me?" he bellowed. "How about the nine years before that?"

"Cole, I—"

"You what, didn't think I had a right to know?"

"That's not it. My parents, they—"

He made a slicing motion with one hand as if to call a halt. "No. You don't get to pin this on someone else. You knew, and you purposely kept it from me."

"I thought you didn't want me anymore. Why would I think you'd care if I was pregnant? At the time, I figured it would be a burden you didn't want."

"So you took it upon yourself to make that decision for me?"

"I swear to God I wanted to tell you. My parents had me on a tight leash. They wouldn't let me out of the house, or near a phone."

"What about now, Jenna? These last nine years? Your parents haven't been with you this whole time."

"I know you don't believe me. But I was going to tell you tonight."

"After we had sex or before?"

She continued to stare at the floor. "I wasn't trying to hide it from you."

"It sure looks that way to me. You were waiting until right before she got here…until you couldn't put it off any longer. What, did you figure once I saw her, I would know? I'll bet if you hadn't come back to Texas for business, ten more years would have gone by, and I still wouldn't have known. Isn't that right?"

Her deceit this time baked the cake. Unbelievable. The nerve of this woman. He shouldered past Jenna, disgusted. "The guest bedroom is down the hall. I have a few extra shirts in the dresser. You can use one to sleep in."

She called to him while he stalked down the hall.

He threw his hand up and kept walking.

****

Jenna opened her eyes to unfamiliar surroundings. After a moment, it became apparent she'd spent the night in Cole's guest bedroom. She sat up, glancing around in a panic, attention darting around for the alarm clock she thought had been spotted on the nightstand last night. Thank God it was only nine a.m. There would be enough time to make it to the airport without being late.

Yawning, she strolled down the hall to the bathroom. After doing her business, she stared in the mirror. The reflection was the face of a woman who looked a wreck—but not nearly as messy as she had made things between her and Cole.

You should have told him a long time ago.

Why, so he could have just reacted this way sooner? Cole had been right. Using her parents as a scapegoat for not telling the truth was a copout. Even if they made it difficult, it had been up to her to make the right decision. She had been wrong for keeping the pregnancy from him.

But they needed to talk before picking up her daughter and parents at the airport. Emily wasn't to blame, and they should be adult enough to ensure she would be kept out of any drama caused by this. Surely, Cole would agree to that much. Once their daughter left, he would be free to fully despise her. And she was sure he would.

Can you blame him? Jenna's heart sank. They had come so far, worked through so many barriers to get to this point. Now it was ruined, all in one dreadful night because something so unforgivable had been hidden from him. Jenna doubted he'd ever get past it. And what could she do with her grief now that she was falling in love with him all over again? Tears slid down her face. If she spent too much time reflecting on losing Cole for the second time, she'd fall completely apart. She dried her eyes, convincing herself to be strong. There was Emily to think about, and in fewer than two hours she'd be climbing off the plane. That little girl couldn't see her like this.

She stepped out of the bathroom and trekked to the kitchen in search of coffee. The house was quiet. Cole must still be asleep. If he didn't wake before long, the unpleasant task of stirring him out of bed would be necessary. And she'd bet he was still pissed as hell.

Stepping into the kitchen, she was relieved to see a high-end coffee maker sitting on the counter. Jenna took a mug from the top cupboard and grabbed a pod from the basket. The sound of paper crinkling caused her to turn toward the dining room. There, sitting at the table was a strange man in uniform reading the newspaper. She almost dropped the sugar bowl.

"Good morning, Ms. Langley," he said, giving her a thorough once over. "I'm Officer Adams, and I'll be your escort for today."

Peering down to discover in horror, the only clothes on her body were a pair of underwear and Cole's oversized T-shirt, she tugged on the material to cover as much as possible. "Where's Cole?"

"He left earlier this morning."

"What about my car?"

The officer hitched a thumb over his shoulder. "Out in the driveway."

"Good. I need to go back and get my clothes."

"That won't be necessary. I gathered your things this morning on my way here. You'll find them in the living room."

"You went through my belongings?"

"I figured you'd want more to wear today than a T-shirt and underwear."

How cute. With that, she dashed out of the kitchen, heading in the direction of the living room. And just as he said, her suitcases were on the floor.

She carried them into the guest bedroom and rifled through the items, and must admit, the guy had done a good job of packing everything a girl needed, even having gathered a bag of toiletries along with her curling iron, makeup, perfumes, and jewelry. He must have a wife.

After showering and getting ready, Jenna wandered back into the bedroom and slipped on her high heels. And then she roamed into the kitchen., finally ready for that coffee.

He sat at the table, reading his paper. She placed the pod into the holder, shutting it, and peered over at him. "I'm sorry, I forgot your name."

"Just call me Joe."

"Well, Joe, I'm impressed at your packing skills. You seemed to know exactly what I needed. Do you have a wife?"

He grinned, folding the paper, and setting it on the table. "And three beautiful daughters."

That explained it. "Thank you."

"You're welcome."

"Would you like another cup of coffee?" she asked, adding sugar and cream to hers.

"No, thanks. I'm on my second cup now."

"I have to pick my daughter and parents up at the airport in forty-five minutes. They don't yet know what's going on here. So I was hoping we could take separate cars, and you could follow behind me this time. I don't want to alarm them. And it would give me a chance to explain everything."

He raised an eyebrow. "Cole is picking them up at the airport."

"What?" She wanted to shriek, tear at her hair.

Joe nodded. "I'm guessing he didn't tell you."

Anger coiled ever tighter. "No. He didn't."

Jenna rushed into the living room where she'd left the phone last night, picked it up, and dialed Cole's number. Her pulse pounded with fury waiting for him to answer. Boy, was he ever going to get it this time. Who did he think he was? It rang several times before going to voicemail, and it only added to her level of lividness. *That son of a bitch.*

She called Amanda and got the same, and then tossed the phone on the table. It was unbelievable Cole had gone this far. He didn't bother to even discuss it with her. Just took it upon himself to do something as reckless as this.

She'd wait for him to get back. And when he did, he was going to have hell to pay.

****

The killer slipped off his toolbelt, setting it on the dusty, plywood floor of the renovated house he'd been working on. It couldn't be later than ten a.m., and the hot, Texas sun beat down as if summer was in full swing. Eighty-five degrees in March with no sign of wind. A few days ago, it had been a high of sixty-two and windy as hell. He shook his head, wiping away sweat. The weather in this state was subject to change at the drop of a hat.

Working alone gave him the luxury of taking a break when and for whatever length of time he wanted. There was no boss man on the job to answer to, no time clock to punch. The killer headed to his vehicle, turned the air conditioner to full blast, and snatched a bottle of water from the cooler sitting on the passenger's seat. Concentrating on the task at hand with so many thoughts swimming around his brain had not been easy. A new and foolproof plan to capture Jenna was in order, but none were coming to mind. And mulling over it for countless hours hadn't helped.

He grabbed his phone and surfed Jenna's social media account again. Perhaps he'd missed something during the last search. Combing through the entries, it was obvious no new postings had been published from her. After last night's failed execution, he was sure there wouldn't be any either. The bitch would steer away from advertising any recent and personal information on the internet. If she didn't have the good sense to take that step, Cole would have undoubtedly seen to it.

Exploring her friends list took him to a name that stood out like a neon sign. *Emily Rainwater.* Heart in his throat, the killer immediately clicked on her picture, bringing up the profile of this Rainwater girl. Her last name was a dead giveaway. And even though she favored Jenna, a reflection of Cole could be seen in that face. *I'll be damned.* Jenna had a daughter, but not just anyone's child...Cole's offspring.

The shock of that information stole his breath. As much as the killer had eavesdropped on Cole throughout the years, how could this evidence have escaped him? And then realization struck with the might of an earthquake. Because Cole had no bloody idea. That little bitch that broke his son's heart years ago and then abandoned him, had been hiding one helluva secret all this time.

Emily Rainwater was an attractive kid and appeared to be around eight or nine years old. A golden retriever sat in the profile picture with the girl. Her small arms were laced around the animal's neck. How cute. She must adore the dog. He sneered. Love was a wasted emotion. It only left people vulnerable. Those who opened themselves up to such weak feelings paid the ultimate price. That had been a lesson learned long ago after what his wife did to him. He would never go back there again. Being reborn was the best thing that ever happened.

He clicked on the child's recent posts and hit paydirt right away. *Me, Grandma, and Grandpa are going to Texas tomorrow to see Momma.*

Is that so? The wheels churned furiously in his mind. This unexpected, new development had the potential to change everything. Amazing how circumstances could go from somber to promising so quickly. This was just the break he needed. Of course, it would take some masterful planning, but the perfect opportunity to pull this off just came knocking.

Euphoria pulsed through him. He was back in the game again. He needed to leave the jobsite and return later to finish out the day. Now he had a lot of eavesdropping that must be done before meeting his granddaughter.

****

Cole strolled through the airport, approaching gate nineteen. They should be coming off the airplane in a few more minutes. The decision had been made last night after tossing and turning for over two hours, he would be the one to pick them up. So, he made a call to Amanda this morning after finding her number in Jenna's phone and laid out the details of the murder case. If it had been left up to Jenna to warn her mother, the woman would have had no idea what she was stepping into.

Even though he harbored a strong dislike for Amanda Langley due to her keeping him and Jenna separated and hiding the pregnancy from him, he couldn't reconcile with how unfair it would be to allow Jenna's mom to come to Texas without knowing the danger she might be facing. It was only fair to have given her the option to stay in Georgia.

But the old witch would have none of it. After hearing about the attack on Jenna, she still insisted on coming. For their safety, Cole decided it best he pick them up. If Jenna knew of his plans, she would have only given him a hard time. And he wasn't about to let her come along and risk her welfare after what happened last night. Jenna wouldn't like it. But she'd get over it.

Passengers shuffled down the tarmac, and Cole waited with bated breath. Discovering last night he had a daughter caused a mixture of elation and confusion. And now that the anticipation of seeing her built, butterflies fluttered through his stomach. During the conversation with Amanda, it had been mentioned he knew the truth about Emily. She didn't have much to say, but he made it clear no one would break the news to the girl except him and Jenna. It was their right. Amanda had already done enough by being the responsible party that kept Emily away from her father.

Jenna's parents stepped out of the throng, appearing ten years older than the last time he saw them. His breath caught when he saw the child positioned between them. Long, auburn hair like Jenna's and the same oval face. But she had his eyes and nose. He approached, barely feeling his legs move beneath him. "Hello, Amanda."

Giving no smile in return, she stood there, stone-faced as always. Lifting her chin, she issued a tight, "Hello, Cole."

He nodded at Robert, Jenna's father. The man gave a half smile that spoke volumes to his discomfort. Fitting, Cole decided.

He knelt in front of his daughter. "And you must be Emily."

She grinned sheepishly. "Are you Cole?"

"Yes, sweetheart, I am. It's nice to meet you."

"Is my Momma gonna be all right?"

"She is going to be fine. After all, she has me to look after her."

She smiled again. "She says you're a good detective."

"Well, I try."

"Do you have a gun?"

He laughed, peering down at the firearm in his holster. "All detectives have guns, Emily. But we are very responsible with them."

"What about a cop car? Do you have one of those?"

He stood and grinned at her. "I sure do. I even

brought it here, just to pick you up today."

"Cool," she said, her eyes lighting up.

He fixed his attention on Jenna's parents. "I've rented a room at the inn for you. You'll be safe there. Officer Reed is assigned with the duty of seeing to your security. He will always be with you but won't get in the way. He's also available to chauffeur you around wherever you need to go. I'll be dropping you two off at the hotel, and then taking Emily to see her mom."

Amanda spoke up. "I don't think—"

Cole cut her off. "I work in law enforcement. She will be safer with me than anyone else." He moved closer to Amanda and said under his breath, "Don't you think you've kept her from me long enough?"

Amanda directed her attention away, a passive expression on her face, saying nothing.

Cole backed off, satisfied the time was soon coming when she'd be made to answer for her actions. But not now. Not in front of his daughter.

He glanced down as Emily slipped her hand in his. "Can I ride up front with you, Cole?"

His heart filled with warmth. "Sure, you can."

The phone in his holder rang. Cole checked the number. It was Jenna again. He silenced the call. After what she did to him, the woman could sit at the house and stew in her misery.

Chapter Eleven

Jenna continued to pace the floor. It had been over two hours since she learned Cole had left for the airport. Although calmer now, she was still fuming at his actions. How many times had she called him just to have Cole ignore the attempts? He had been doing it purposely, and Jenna damn well knew it.

When he and Emily finally strolled through the door, Jenna glared at Cole. Before she could say a word, the girl bounded toward her. "Momma, I got to ride in a cop car!"

Jenna pasted on a smile and embraced Emily. "That's awesome." She dropped a kiss on top of her head. "How did you like the plane ride?"

"It was a little scary. But Grandma held my hand and promised it would be all right."

She stared at Cole who stood by the door, remembering how much he hated planes, too. And judging by his expression, the same thought must have occurred to him.

She drew Emily away. "Why don't you head into the bathroom down the hall and freshen up after the long flight? Cole and I need a little adult time, okay?"

"Aw, Momma."

"Go on. You need to wash your face and hands."

"Oh, all right."

The minute she disappeared Jenna turned on Cole.

"What do you think you're doing taking off like that without even telling me?"

"You mean the way you did to me ten years ago?"

She turned away, staring at the fireplace in the corner. Her attention rested on a picture sitting on the cherry wood mantle. Cole was dressed in the uniform of a sworn police officer. He smiled handsomely, kneeling with his hands clasped together around one knee, a police flag in the background. "This isn't about that."

"Oh no? If you hadn't left the way you did, things would be a lot different right now. That little girl would know who I am."

She lowered her head, now studying the colorful patterns in the oriental rug, considering how right he was. Guilty as charged. "What did you tell my parents?"

"Everything. If I had left it up to you, they would have boarded that plane without knowing what's going on. As I realize honesty is an unfamiliar concept to you, they had a right to the truth."

"You're not being fair."

"Is the way you treated me your definition of *fair*?"

"I realize how wrong that was. Believe me. But my daughter—"

"Whose daughter?"

She stopped and took a deep breath. "*Our* daughter is innocent in all this. And we need to be patient and take our time explaining you're her father."

"Do you take me for an idiot?"

"So you didn't tell her?"

"Of course not."

Hearing a noise, Jenna peered over to see Emily standing in the middle of the living room. Although she couldn't be sure how much the child had overheard, by the stunned expression on her face, it was obvious she'd listened long enough. "Emily, honey. How long have you been standing there?"

"Is Cole my daddy?"

Jenna's attention wandered to Cole. He lowered his head, stepped over to the couch, and sat down. She nodded and said, "Yes, he is." She took Emily's hand, and settled her in beside Cole, then sat down next to her. "I should have told you long ago."

The child searched her eyes and asked, "Why didn't you?"

She took a moment to reflect, being careful to find the right words. "Have you ever known you should tell somebody something but didn't have the courage? And then, so much time goes by you don't know how to tell them anymore?"

She appeared deep in thought and said, "I think so. Something like that happened to my best friend Chloe. She liked this boy in class but was too afraid to tell him. And she waited so long he got another girlfriend."

"That's a really good example," Jenna told her. "If I'd been smart, I'd have been brave and told you sooner."

"Did you know?" she asked Cole.

He shook his head. "Your momma told me last night."

"So she didn't tell you either?"

When Emily's head swung toward Jenna, Anger swelled in the child's eyes. "That's not very nice what you did."

"You're right. It's not." And it was the truth, whether Jenna liked it or not. This was all her fault.

"You know what I think?" Cole chimed in. "Your momma was a young girl when she got pregnant with you. And her mom and dad were afraid if she told me, I would take her away and they would lose her."

"Would you do that? Take Momma away from them?"

"No. But I think they were worried I would."

Emily frowned, in her eyes was a genuine attempt to understand. "Grandma and Grandpa should have known better."

"Yes. They should have. But they loved your momma so much fear drove them to convince her not to tell me. And when you're as young as your momma had been, your parents have a lot of influence over you. So, I don't think you should be too hard on your mom."

"Then it was Grandma and Grandpa's fault."

"I think they did it out of love," Cole continued. "Sometimes adults make bad decisions because they think they're doing the right thing for someone they care about. And they don't realize their actions can hurt that person later down the road. Do you understand what I'm saying, Emily?"

She nodded. "I get it. I just wish they would have told the truth. It's always the right thing to do."

He chuckled and said, "A child after my own heart."

She stared at him, confused. "What does that mean?"

He smiled, patting her hand. "It means I feel the same way."

"Oh."

He ruffled her hair. "I know it's hard. But sometimes we need to consider forgiving people when we know they did things because they thought they were protecting us, even if they hurt us without realizing it."

"I see what you mean. I'll have to think about it."

"Fair enough."

Jenna couldn't believe what just took place. Cole reasoned with Emily in a way she never would have been able to. Did he mean what he said about the influence her parents had and the fact she had been young and naïve enough to have let this happen?

"Someone has a birthday today," Cole said.

"Yep. And Momma said we can go to the zoo and maybe the aquarium too. Ain't that right, Momma?"

"Ain't isn't a word," Jenna reminded her.

"You know," Cole broke in, "I have a friend who owns a horse ranch. He said we can come and ride horses all day if we want. What do you say we pack a lunch and head over there?"

Emily lunged off the couch, excitedly jumping up and down. "Can we, Momma?"

"I don't know. You've never ridden a horse before. What if you fall off?"

"She will be fine. His daughter is home from spring break, and she can teach Emily to ride. They are expecting us."

She glared at him. "You planned this."

"I had a feeling Emily would love it."

"Heck yeah!" The child glanced at him and asked, "Is it okay if I call you Cole?"

He grinned, and then let out a chuckle. "As long as I can call you Emily."

She giggled and he said, "If your mom will pack us a lunch, I'll get your suitcase out of the car. You'll need to dress in a pair of comfortable slacks, okay?"

"Uh-huh." She skipped out of the room.

Jenna asked, "Is Officer Adams coming with us?"

"No. I'll relieve him when I get back from the car."

"Cole?"

He stared to her, showing no emotion.

"Thank you."

"For what?" She could still sense irritation in his voice.

She cleared her throat and peered away. "That thing you did with Emily. I thought it was commendable is all."

He approached the door, opened it, and said tightly, "Well, I'm a commendable kind of guy. Too bad you never noticed."

When he strode out, she did not doubt Cole had not forgiven her.

****

Cole pulled his truck up to the security gate at the Vazquez Ranch. Sam, the guard on duty, beamed when he recognized him. "Hey, Cole. Dario said you might be swinging by. Taking the daughter horse riding, aye?"

Emily rolled down the window in the back seat and poked her head out. "Hi. I'm Emily."

He tipped his cowboy hat to her. "Well, hey there, little lady. My name is Sam."

She giggled.

"Is Dario in by chance?" Cole wanted to know.

"He and Suzy are up at the house."

"See ya later, Sam."

"Y'all have fun."

After Sam opened the gate and they drove through, Emily said, "I never saw a real cowboy before."

"Well, then. You're in for a real treat because there are lots of them here."

"And horses," she squealed.

They rounded the curve leading to the house and as soon as it came into view, Jenna said, "Wow, Cole. This is a mansion. Who are these people?"

"An old friend from back when I used to work for the Fort Worth PD. Dario was one of the best detectives on the force before he retired. His wife, Suzy, is part owner of the family's oil business."

She frowned, her expression awestruck as she took in the extravagant sight of the place. "I can tell. When I look at this place, I feel so underdressed."

"We came to ride, not sip tea and eat cakes."

"Maybe you two did, but not me. I'm not getting on a horse, Cole. I already told you that."

"We'll see about that," he said, parking the truck, and opening the door.

Emily hopped out, impatiently waiting for them.

After Jenna grabbed the lunch basket, they all headed toward the house.

The front door opened, and a young, Latina girl shuffled out dressed in riding gear. "Hi," she said, meeting them at the bottom of the steps.

"How are you doing, Rosa?" Cole asked, grinning, and then introduced everyone. "This is Jenna, and our daughter, Emily. Guys, this is Dario and Suzy's daughter, Rosa."

"Hi, Emily," Rosa said, zeroing in on the girl.

"Hi."

"Do you want to go see the horses?" Rosa asked.

"Can I, Momma?"

"Sure. But no riding until I get there."

Cole glanced at Rosa and winked. Then his attention focused on Jenna. “Rosa is a very experienced rider. She’s been riding the rodeo circuit since she was seven years old. Emily is in very capable hands.”

The thirteen-year-old girl smiled sheepishly. “Yes, ma’am. I’ve been around horses all my life. I won’t let Emily get hurt. I promise.”

“Well, okay. Just be careful, please.”

As they ran off, Cole gazed at Jenna. “You will like Dario and Suzy. They’re two of the most down-to-earth people I know.”

She pursed her lips. “Living in this place? You’re kidding, right?”

“You’ll see.” He led her up the steps and through the front door.

The butler stood by, ready to take their jackets. They handed them over, and Dario strolled into the room. He grinned at Cole. “Hey, my brother. How have you been?”

Seeing him reminded Cole how long it had been since he had taken the time to visit friends. “Hanging in there.”

Dario laughed, marched over, and gave Cole a man hug, clapping him on the back. “I was tickled pink when you called this morning. I told Suzy she was going to have to take the day off. It’s a rare treat when we get to see your face.”

“What, this ugly mug?”

“This guy is as handsome as a devil. He just doesn’t know it,” Dario said to Jenna, then he glanced at Cole. “Aren’t you going to introduce us?”

“Jenna, this is Dario. And Dario this is Jenna.”

Dario stuck out his hand, and when Jenna offered

hers, he kissed it. "Well, Cole, you never told me you were hiding such a gem. Pardon an old man for saying, ma'am, but you are the loveliest thing."

Pink inflamed Jenna's cheeks.

Cole didn't doubt Dario's words. He was right. The woman was gorgeous. When they dated as teens, he always felt like a king with her on his arm.

"My, my. Look what the cat dragged in."

Cole turned around to see Suzy standing a few feet away. "Hey, there, Ms. Suzy," he said, crossing the room and hugging her. "Still looking beautiful, I see."

"Oh, stop. We both know I'm just an old hen. But this young lady here," she said, walking toward Jenna, "now that's another story entirely." Suzy glared at her husband. "Do you remember when I used to be this radiant, Dario?"

"Darlin', you've always been a diamond."

She chuckled and said to Jenna, "He has to say that cuz I'm married to him."

Dario spoke up. "You see? I can't even compliment this woman and get away with it."

Cole grinned. "That's because she knows what a hound dog you are."

"You know it," Suzy retorted. "Well, come on, you two. Are we here to ride horses or bullshit all afternoon? Jeffery's already got the horses saddled up," she said, leading them through a few rooms and out a back door, toward the horse stables.

Cole discreetly stared at Jenna as they made their way. Confusion about his feelings for her only added to the frustration. God help him, the passion was still as strong today as it had been ten years ago. No matter what happened, he would never get that out of his blood. But hiding the pregnancy of their child ran deep. Cole had a right to know, and she'd taken that away from him. How does someone forgive a person for something like that? Because of it, he had lost ten precious years with his daughter. And no apology in the world could give that time back to him.

Yet was it possible to move on without her a second time? Within the short time she'd been in Texas, she had already crawled right back into Cole's heart and consumed his mind. Did he have the strength to see her walk out all over again?

As they hit the entrance to the horse stable, Jenna became fidgety. Nervousness emanated from her. By all appearances, the last thing she wanted to do was climb on a horse. He was going to have to ride with her and ease the fear away.

"You've ridden before, right?" she whispered.

"I was a little scared too the first time. But once you get past that, you wouldn't believe the freedom you feel while riding. I'll go with you if that helps."

He could already see the relief on her face. Might as well resign to being fix-it man today. Hey, when you're on a roll.

The stable hand showed them to their horses, and he explained to the guy they would both be riding together today. "Her name is Fancy," he told Jenna, standing in front of a brown mare. "She's not a racing horse, so the ride should be gentle. Would you like to pet her?"

"Sure."

Jenna lifted her hand to the horse's head. The mare neighed, closing her eyes, appearing to enjoy the attention. "Hi, Fancy," she said, continuing to pet the horse. "You are a beautiful girl."

Watching Jenna's pleasure as she explored the large animal gave Cole a kind of unselfish satisfaction. It was as if his happiness depended on hers. If he couldn't bring joy into this woman's life, there would be none for him. "You think you're up for riding her?"

"I'll give it a try."

"That's what I want to hear." Cole grabbed the horse by the reins and walked it out of the stable. He pointed to the stirrup. "Put your foot right there, and swing your leg over."

"Are you sure she won't run off before you climb on with me?"

"I'm positive."

She stared at the horse, undecided.

"It's okay. I've ridden this horse before, and she's steady as can be. She won't move until I give the order. Just climb on, and I'll be right behind you."

He helped Jenna get her foot into the stirrup and told her to swing her leg over. It took a few tries, but it was a proud moment when she finally achieved it. He mounted the horse, peering back, saying, "Hold on to my waist."

He closed his eyes the moment her arms slipped around him. Jenna's touch awakened something in him that sent Cole's head reeling. It took an unbelievable amount of strength to keep the sexual urges in check as he tapped the sides of the horse with his heels, giving the mare a command to trot.

Jenna held on tight as they circled the stable and rode out into the meadow. It had been far too long since he'd climbed on the back of a horse. And God, it was amazing. Cole glanced back to see Jenna's hair blowing in the breeze, and he noticed her grip loosened a bit. She was relaxing some.

"How is it?" he asked over his shoulder.

"It's kind of nice."

"Are you ready to go a little faster?"

"I'm not sure. How much faster?"

"Do you trust me?"

"Now you're scaring me."

"I won't let you fall off. Do you trust me?"

"Yes."

"Good." With that, he slapped his heels a little harder against the horse, and the animal picked up speed.

"This is something, Cole."

"You like it, huh?"

"Not bad."

"Hold on," he said, urging the mare to go faster. They broke into a hard run and headed out to the bottom ten acres.

He slowed the pace as they approached the pond and circled halfway around it. Once the horse came to a full stop, Cole dismounted and helped Jenna out of the saddle.

He strolled to the water's edge, taking in the warmth of the sun and the cool breeze blowing against his face.

Jenna sidled up, only a few inches away. "It's nice, isn't it?"

He nodded, peering out across the way. "I used to come here all the time. Helped me get away, you know, from the world." *And my tormenting thoughts of you.*

"I can understand why. How long have you known Dario and Suzy?"

"I met Dario when I was a rookie. He got me into the investigation unit. Took me off the beat."

"I didn't know you ride. You're good at it."

The way the sunlight danced across her skin was just too much. He cupped her cheek, and whispered, hoarsely, "Come here to me, Jenna."

The moment she leaned into him, he took her lips, hopelessly lost in the intoxicating taste of her. There was an undeniable war raging inside between keeping his distance and surrendering like a fool whenever she got close. How much longer could he go on this way? The woman aroused him with just a glance. His body was on fire in her presence, and nothing on God's green earth stood a chance of putting out the flames. At least not until he found himself buried deep inside her. And even that would do nothing more than leave him wanting the woman again and again.

As she molded against him, her hand slid to the back of his head, fingers entwining in his hair. And then horse hooves drummed in the distance.

He broke the kiss, backing away from the hunger in her eyes. Cole needed to come to his senses and stop torturing himself. But it was too late. That was no longer an option.

Two horses approached from over the horizon. Emily and Rosa appeared over the hill, sitting high in the saddle. "Oh my God," Jenna said, "I think Emily is on that horse by herself."

His chest filled with pride. "Has she always been this brave at home?"

Chapter Twelve

The sun was setting low by the time Cole and Jenna headed back home. The two girls had begged relentlessly for Emily to spend the night. Although he recalled the skepticism on Jenna's face considering all that had been going on, the Vazquez Ranch was one of the safest places his daughter could be. Dario had been a trained police officer and investigator. And the place was surrounded by armed security guards around the clock. Nothing got into the ranch without Dario's knowledge and approval. She would be safer there than she would be with Jenna. After enough convincing, her mother finally gave in—but only after Cole promised to pick her up first thing in the morning.

It had been the best day Cole could ever remember having. But the fondest memory of all had been when they had settled in with the girls, Dario, and Suzy to have a picnic by the pond. It was at that time Emily jumped in Cole's lap, threw her arms around his neck, kissed him on the cheek, and said *thank you* for the best birthday she'd ever had.

But now that they were heading home, Cole regretted the night would end having dinner with her parents. But he'd been the one who made the arrangements. Now that his daughter would not be attending. The time had come for them to answer for what they'd done.

According to the truck radio, it was six thirty p.m. when they pulled up at his house. Getting out, he reminded Jenna they only had an hour to shower and get ready before arriving at the restaurant.

Cole allowed Jenna to use the master shower, while he used the one in the guest bathroom. Now, sitting on the couch and waiting for her to finish seemed like an eternity. A memory hit Cole, and he chuckled inwardly. How many times had she kept him waiting at her parent's house, while she had been upstairs getting ready for their date? At least now he was in the comfort of his home, and not listening to her father ramble on about duck hunting, while Amanda shot him *you're not good enough for my daughter* expressions from across the room.

She finally ambled into the living room. The sight of the woman stole his breath. She was beautiful. The ponytail from today was gone. Her long hair fell around tan shoulders. The dress she chose was not provocative but displayed her curves nicely. He swallowed, realizing it was going to be a long night.

The restaurant was twenty minutes away, and they arrived right on time. Knowing Amanda's finicky nature, reservations had been made at the best steak house in McKinney. He cursed under his breath getting out of the truck. What he should have done was taken them to the Waffle House. The sight of her eating cheap fries swimming in ketchup and a greasy hamburger would have made his day. Although Cole may have been a lot of things, unfortunately, vindictive wasn't one of them tonight.

Yet, as he walked around to open Jenna's door, a wave of satisfaction reeled through him. This time it would not be like it was when he had been dating their daughter and they held all the cards. They were in Cole's territory and at his mercy. He had the upper hand now.

The maître d' took their coats as they entered and showed them to their reserved table. Jenna's parents were already there. Amanda sipped wine, a few empty glasses sitting on the table in front of her. If Cole had been as condescending as her, he'd have to drink a lot to live with himself too.

The shrew ignored him and sent a fake smile in the direction of her daughter. "It's nice to finally see you, Jenna. I was beginning to wonder if that would ever happen."

"It must have been rough," Cole said, "having been away from her for a whole day."

Amanda appeared shocked he would talk to her that way. "That's not true, Cole. I haven't seen my daughter in quite a few weeks. Have you forgotten?"

"If you hadn't ripped her away from Texas and taken her to Georgia, you wouldn't have that problem, would you?"

"Excuse me?"

"Besides, I think a few weeks is hardly a comparison to nine years, don't you?"

Amanda stood, the woman's face stricken with disbelief. She peered down at her husband. "I told you we shouldn't have come here. This man has no decency," she said, cutting an icy stare in his direction. "And he never has."

Staring at his wife, Robert abandoned his chair. "Amanda, sit. You are making a spectacle of yourself."

"He is the one making a spectacle," she sputtered.

"He owes all of us an apology for his unacceptable behavior."

"Mother." Jenna cut in, appearing angrier than Cole had ever seen her. "If you don't sit down right now, I swear to God you will never see me or your granddaughter ever again."

Whoa. Cole did not know what Jenna's reaction would be when he confronted Amanda tonight. But there was no doubt now where she stood. Pride filled his chest that she finally stood up to this dominating woman.

Amanda retook her seat. " I can't believe all of you are taking his side."

"There aren't any sides, Amanda," Robert told her, sitting back down. "The truth is we robbed this man of knowing his daughter. And that is the most unforgivable thing."

As Cole finally took a seat with Jenna, he was surprised to hear Robert talk this way, yet at the same time relieved at least one of them was willing to own up to what they had done.

Robert faced him. "I know it's of little consolation. And I realize it's too much to ask for your forgiveness, but we are so sorry. I guess in our way we thought we were doing what was best for Jenna. But it is more apparent to me now than ever we hurt her, and you, by ripping you two apart and hiding the pregnancy. What your father did was not your fault. I can see you are a good man, Cole. You didn't deserve that."

After all these years of suffering, Cole felt more vindicated now than he ever could be. Robert was right, it was too much to ask for him to forgive them, at least right now. But the man opened the door, and forgiveness became possible because of that.

"I appreciate it more than you know," he said, and then added in the famous words of his daughter, "*I'll have to think about it.*"

****

Even though it hadn't been the greatest experience to sit across from Jenna's scowl-faced mother while trying to eat, there had been a decent conversation among Robert, him, and Jenna. In all, the meeting was a success. In terms of his daughter, they knew where Cole stood. Forgiving them would take time. He gave them details of the murder investigation, and they discussed where Emily would stay while in Texas. In the end, they decided the child would visit between the Langleys and her parents. But of course, Emily would always have the security of an officer with her when she was with anyone other than Cole.

Jenna broke the silence as they drove to his home. "I was thinking. Since I'm a business consultant, I can do that from anywhere. I know Emily would love to spend as much time with you as possible. And if I came back to Texas permanently, she'd be able to do that."

He glanced at her. "Are you serious?

She smiled and nodded.

"That would be amazing."

"Did you see her today? She rode like a pro."

"A chip off the old block."

"Thank you, Cole, for taking us there. I don't remember the last time I saw her have that much fun."

"And what about you?"

"I had a great time. I didn't realize how enjoyable that would be."

"Ya know, I've had my eye on a ten-acre lot in

Hunt County. I've talked to a real estate buddy of mine about it, and he seems to think it would be a good investment. I was considering putting a down payment on it. I think it would be a great place for a ranch."

"Really?"

"I always wanted a few horses, and Emily could sharpen her riding skills."

"I think it's a great idea."

"Yeah?'

"Yeah."

She cleared her throat. "Listen, I know you probably don't want to deal with this right now, but I have to get something off my chest."

"If this has anything to do with you not telling me about Emily, I really— "

"You were right."

Not expecting that, he stared at her.

"What you said last night. I can't blame my parents for this any longer. I knew it was wrong. And I should have done something about it. It's true, they made it difficult for me." She peered out the window. "Sometimes I hate them for what they did. It wasn't just you they stole something precious from. They stole my whole world from me too. You were everything to me. And when they refused to let me see you, I felt dead inside. There were days I felt disgusted I was still breathing. Then came the morning sickness, and I knew I was pregnant. I was stupid enough to think when I told my mother she would realize how wrong this was and agree we should be together, as a family. But that's not what happened. It only made her want to get me away from you more. That's when she convinced my father to leave Texas."

Ten years had come and gone. During that time, Cole never considered she might feel that way. "Jenna," he said, a crack in his voice. "You were seventeen. They are your parents and as such were in control of your life."

She shook her head. "No. The thing is, I let them do it. I should have stood up for myself. I should have told them to go to hell. You don't know how close I came to running away. The only thing that stopped me was I thought you didn't love me anymore. And I figured I would have no place to go."

The reality of the situation hadn't set in on him until she said that. "God, Jenna. I would have moved the earth for you, do you know that?"

"I wish I would have."

And Cole wished he would have realized she still loved him. If that had been the case Amanda and Robert Langley wouldn't have stopped him from crashing through their door and stealing away with Jenna. But that wasn't the way it went down. Now all they had to show for it were too many regrets to count.

Cole turned into the driveway, plucked the key from the ignition, and opened the door. She still gazed out the window. "It's late," he said, "Let's go inside."

He took Jenna by the hand and led her through the door. But they didn't stop in the living room. Heart in his throat, they walked down the hall to the bedroom.

Once inside, he didn't say a word, simply led Jenna to his bed, and unzipped her dress. She stepped out of the garment and unlatched her shoes, kicking them off. Cole's fingers worked to free the strap of her bra. It no sooner hit the ground then he had the woman he loved on the bed, straddling her.

He stared at Jenna, lifting her hand to his lips, kissing each finger one by one. Judging by the burning desire in those blue eyes, the gentle caress was having the same seductive effect it had so many times before when he had her naked and willing on the seat of his truck. As he leaned down to take Jenna's lips, the warm, sweet taste of the woman urged him on. He descended to the softness of two creamy breasts, tongue swirling around a swollen nipple. Her reaction sent a tidal wave of liquid heat coursing through him. She closed her eyes with a slightly open mouth, and he knew from experience it was a sign she wanted more.

This time nothing would stop him from giving it to her. His hand traveled down Jenna's stomach, past silky hips, and Cole slid his fingers under her panties. The moment he touched her, slipping inside, she inhaled sharply. The torment continued, moving his fingers in a circular motion deep iside her, and she cried out.

She interrupted their lovemaking by unbuttoning Cole's shirt, sliding it down the rest of his body and tossing it aside. With eyes burning into him, her hands traced over every muscle of his torso. He'd waited so long to feel her touch once again on his bare skin and his eyes closed against the desire ripping through him. She cut a searing path down to his abdomen, resting her hand just above his jeans. As soon as Jenna found Cole's hardened shaft, a sigh burst from his lips. She cupped him, massaging, applying more pressure, and just when the brink was drawing near, she unbuttoned his jeans, releasing the zipper.

Over the years, he lost count of the many nights spent lying awake longing for her, remembering all the times they'd made love. And tonight, here she was, ready and eager in his bed. Yet he knew the moment he drove into her, it would all be over quickly.

He climbed off Jenna, sliding her panties down, and throwing them to the side. After spreading her legs, the kisses started from the ankle, dragging to the calf, up to Jenna's knee, and softly nibbling the inside of her thigh. Then he kissed her clitoris, and his tongue lapped, moving in a figure-eight motion.

"Oh, God!" she cried, hands going to his hair, and gently grabbing two fistfuls. He stopped for a moment, running his tongue around her clitoris, teasing Jenna. And from the expression on the woman's face, it was working. Cole's tongue found her wetness again, and the torturous stroking continued until she was about to orgasm. Then Cole stood, slipping off his jeans.

She stared at his nakedness, and he couldn't deny how much it turned him on. Then Cole climbed on top of her, driving his shaft deep inside her at the same moment he captured her lips. Her hands slid down Cole's back, settling around the hips, and thrusting his hard cock further inside.

Cole rode her slowly at first, relishing every moment. He'd forgotten how amazing she felt. And he feared if he thrust too quickly, the climax would come just as fast.

But she was having none of it and started calling out, "Oh, God, Cole, harder. More. Give me every inch."

And he did, picking up the pace, slamming himself into her, until hearing Jenna scream.

All at once, his muscles tightened, and he let loose. When the last wave dissipated, he gazed into Jenna's eyes, leaning down and kissing the tip of her nose.

"God, woman, I think you killed me."

She smiled and pinched his arm.

"Ouch. What was that for?"

"Just checking. You're still alive."

"Ha ha. So would you like a glass of wine before we do this again?"

"I'd love one. This time, I think I'll get on top."

His brows raised. "Let's make that a quick glass then."

****

The killer lifted the binoculars as the little girl named Emily got out of Cole's truck. His son led the child to the entrance of the inn, where a police officer waited to take her by the hand and lead the girl inside. Since running across Emily's social media account, the killer had spent his time scoping out their activities, following all of them around. Yesterday afternoon he had headed to his son's house and was lucky enough to catch him returning with the girl.

He smiled wickedly, thankful for the internet and its digital footprint. That had made it possible to track Jenna and Emily down to begin with.

The killer dropped the binoculars into his lap. Convincing Emily to come with him willingly would pave the way to lure Jenna to him without using violence, and that would keep the bitch from tapping into her psychic abilities. He sat quietly for a moment, envisioning the plan. It was one of his best. It would bring Jenna right to his doorstep. Then he'd get rid of her, and the shitstorm she had created would be nothing more than a distant memory.

But disguises would have to be used, especially now that a sketch of his face was plastered all over the news. It was a good thing the boss man never watched TV. And he worked alone, removing the possibility of a co-worker reporting to police the resemblance between him and the drawing.

Cole pulled away, and he figured the child's grandparents must be staying with her at the hotel. A little bit of covert spying revealed Jenna was not here with her daughter. The bitch was at work with a police escort. Excitement ran through him. The child would be easy pickings.

He punched the steering wheel, hooting out loud, reeling from the amazement of his wit. His son may be foolish enough to believe he could keep Jenna safe, but Cole didn't realize that Papa had an ace up his sleeve. *Yes, indeed.* Starting up his vehicle, he pointed it toward the highway. His next stop would be a local convenience store to pick up a burner phone.

****

After dropping Emily with Amanda and Robert, and seeing them all off safely with Officer Reed, Cole strode into the precinct with a renewed sense of purpose. The night spent with Jenna had been amazing.

Gone was the torture that had been living inside him for ten long years. Having Jenna back in his life again, making love to her brought new meaning to it. Fatherhood changed everything. It offered a future Cole never thought imaginable. And he planned to spend as much time as possible getting to know his beautiful daughter, as well as making up lost time with the woman he loved, and always had.

"What's got you in such a good mood?" Gibbs wanted to know, standing in front of Cole's desk. And then an expression of understanding crossed his face.

"Jenna's staying at your house. Never mind. I can figure it out."

"And that's—"

"None of my business. I already know. But her involvement in this case is. You were going to tell me all about that, remember?"

Cole stared at him, coming to a decision how much he should reveal.

Gibbs said, "Whatever you are thinking of not telling me, I'd advise you to reconsider. I'm on a need-to-know basis, man. We are chasing a killer. And we have to rely on each other."

Cole frowned. "All right, but it's going to sound crazy."

"I can handle it."

He sighed. "Jenna's clairvoyant. She's had visions of some of the murders."

Gibbs appeared incredulous. "And you believe that woo-woo shit?"

"I didn't until she led me right to the car our guy set on fire. She knew about the last two murders and the kidnappings."

"And you're telling me this now?"

"Would you have believed me if I'd have told you earlier?"

"Hell no."

"I didn't believe it myself to begin with. But every one of her descriptions has been dead on."

"So you think she saw our guy breaking into her place in a vision?"

"Yeah. As crazy as that sounds."

"What makes you think the assault has some personal connection to you?"

"Because I think we're dealing with a copycat of my father."

"What?"

"Look." Cole opened a drawer and plucked out the recent sketch of the killer. He laid it on the desk, then grabbed another photo and placed it next to the drawing. "This," he said, pointing to the suspect, "is our perp. And this other guy is my father, Derek Rainwater." Cole motioned toward the photo. "Do you see a resemblance? I noticed it the other night when you texted me the sketch."

"Where did you get that?" Gibbs wanted to know, referring to the picture of his father.

"Out of the evidence room. I was rifling through my father's case."

"There is a resemblance."

"Damn right there is?"

"It doesn't prove it's a copycat?"

"He dresses just like my father. The guy even wears dog tags. And he has the same MO as Derek Rainwater."

"You've been investigating this angle?"

"If it walks and quacks like a duck…"

"You're thinking this guy's been researching you?"

"Everything we know about him tells us he is an experienced killer. He knows how to cover his tracks, get rid of evidence, and keep from leaving DNA behind. This is a game to him. He's upping the ante by bringing me into it. The bastard is doing that through Jenna."

"But how would he—"

"I don't know how he knew we were connected. But he somehow found out we used to date. That shit at the rental was no chance occurrence. The perp deliberately targeted her because he thought I'd get the message that he was making this personal."

He could tell the wheels in Gibbs' mind were spinning by the distant expression in his eyes. "Maybe you're on to something here."

"Any results from the Perez rape kit?"

"No. Nothing from the lab yet."

Cole doubted it was worth wasting his breath to ask, but… "How about the list of drivers? Have we exhausted the names yet?"

Channing passed by Cole's office, then backtracked, stopping outside the threshold. "I heard you mention the list. We've run down all but one. It's a deceased female, Julie Hartness. Died at the age of forty-two in 2009. Her last known address is McKinney. I'm about to head out there and see if any of the family members still live there."

"Tell you what," Cole said, deciding on a whim he'd check it out himself. Besides, there wasn't much going on here at the moment. "Bring me the information, and I'll go out there."

"You sure?" Channing asked, with an expression that told Cole handing the assignment to someone else would be heaven. The guy seemed as if he'd had enough of beating the pavement and getting nowhere.

"Yep."

"All right then. Give me a second and I'll round it up for you."

Chapter Thirteen

The killer shoved the last bit of hair beneath the wig and snatched down the visor, staring in the mirror to check his work. The mustache was straight and perfectly matched the blond hair of the fake beard. He missed the goatee already and hated that it had to go. But erasing as much likeness to the guy in the sketch as possible had been a necessary step. Satisfied with his appearance, he stepped out of his vehicle.

Once inside, he headed straight for the front desk and said to the young woman manning the phones, "Hello. I'm the new janitor hire, and they forgot to tell me where the staff quarters are."

She hardly glanced at him and pointed down the hall. "Go through the double doors at the end. You'll see the suite on your right."

When he entered the room, a few employees were gathering items and filling their caddies. "Excuse me," he said to the skinny girl with black hair. "They just hired me for the janitor position. I need to know where the uniform and supplies are."

She appeared annoyed. "Steve is over that department. He didn't show you where to go?"

"Look, it's my first day and I don't want to get a late start. If you can help me out."

She sighed, and said, "Follow me. I'll take you to the supply room."

They trekked to a room in the back, and she pointed to a shelf filled with folded garments. "Go ahead and grab a uniform from here. Have they given you a name tag yet?"

He feigned ignorance, shaking his head.

"I swear, nobody does anything around here." She opened a drawer and plucked out a blank name tag with the company's logo on it. "This will have to do until they get you one printed."

He took it from her, and she led him into another room. "Here are the supplies. Just grab a cart and a mop bucket. You can change in there," she said, pointing toward a small bathroom."

He nodded his appreciation.

She stalked off, complaining about the incompetence of this Steve person.

When she was out of sight the killer moved quickly, tugging the one-piece uniform over his clothes, and pinning on the nametag. Inspecting the cart, he was pleased it seemed tall enough to offer decent cover.

He snatched out the burner phone and called the front desk. The time had come to flush Emily out of whatever room her grandparents were staying in.

A grin the size of Texas stretched across his face when the desk clerk answered. He said, "Listen to me very closely. I've planted a bomb in the basement. You have twenty minutes to evacuate the building before it detonates. I suggest you start moving."

He got off the phone and slipped on a pair of gloves, using a cloth from the supply cart to wipe fingerprints from the phone, and any areas of the cart that had been touched. Then he stuffed the piece of material in his pocket and headed toward the bank of elevators, tossing the electronic device in a trash can along the way.

As he waited, the chaos was already underway. Hotel staff hurriedly ran here and there. Loud chatter ensued. Phones rang off the hook. Within minutes, the elevator hall buttons lit up and he took off his gloves, shoving them into his pocket. It was showtime.

He stood in the background as people filed out of both elevators in a near panic.

When the elevator on the right opened for the third time, Emily Rainwater stood behind her grandparents and an officer. He slipped into the crowd, as hordes of people from different directions meshed, forming a mob, heading toward the nearest exit.

The second he noticed the officer and her grandparents distracted by the size of the gathering, the killer rushed in and grabbed the girl's hand, weaving his way in the opposite direction quickly.

He hollered over his shoulder, "It's okay, Emily. I'm Cole's dad, your grandfather. And he sent me to make sure you got out safely."

The child tugged on his hand. "What about my grandma and grandpa?"

"The officer is taking care of them. But your dad was really worried about you. He didn't want that bad man who attacked your mom to kidnap you. So, he sent me to take you to the police station where he is, okay?"

"I don't know. Are you sure? How come he never mentioned you?"

He stopped for a moment to peer back at Emily. Then reassured her with a smile. "I work at the police station with your father. I've been undercover here, dressed like a janitor. Your dad sent me to keep you safe. But we must hurry, Emily. You're in danger. Cole is waiting for us at the station. And I promised him I wouldn't let anything happen to you."

The child's expression lightened a bit. "Isn't the exit back that way?"

"I know a better way out of here. Trust me. I already hatched an escape route just in case something like this happened."

The killer rushed the child down a long corridor, and out a side exit that opened into a deserted parking lot. They approached his vehicle, and he encouraged her to get inside quickly.

Hesitating, she took a few steps back. "You don't look like my dad."

He was so close to the child the urge to grab her, throwing her in the back seat was almost impossible to resist. But he couldn't commit violent acts or risk Jenna tapping into her psychic abilities. And the time was not right just yet for her to get wise to his plan. He forced a smile. "It's a disguise. All undercover cops wear them. Didn't your dad ever tell you that?"

The child was unmoved, peering over her shoulder as if she considered bolting.

The killer threw up his hands and strode around to the driver's side. "I can call your dad to come get you." He climbed in and rolled down the passenger's window, leaning over the steering wheel to examine her. "But he'll be mad."

She munched on her lip. "How can you prove you're my grandpa?"

He opened the glove box and plucked out the photo of Cole and Jenna. "Here's a picture I took of your mom and dad when they were teenagers."

She cautiously stepped forward to examine it. "Wow, they were young."

"Emily, we need to leave. I think the killer is here. I believe he set the bomb as a way of trying to get you out of your room. I've got to get you to the police station."

She finally nodded, opened the door, and settled into the seat, although he could tell she was still skeptical.

When they pulled out of the parking lot and headed toward the highway ramp, he couldn't believe how easy that was. Now that the hostage was safely in his vehicle, he could use her as a bargaining chip to bring Jenna to him.

He had no idea what to do with her once Jenna arrived at his house. He didn't like the idea of killing her since she was his granddaughter, but there may not be a choice in the matter. If she ended up seeing too much…

As the killer exited the highway and turned the sports utility vehicle in the direction of his house, he pushed the consideration aside. That bridge would have to be crossed when they came to it. First things first. Time to get her mother out of the way for good.

****

The house where Julie Hartness lived twelve years ago was a ten-thousand-square-foot beauty. Cole passed a fountain in the center of the circle drive and walked across cobblestones heading toward the huge Egyptian statues he imagined would lead to the entrance.

He stood in front of a door twice as tall as him and rang the buzzer.

After a few minutes, the lock disengaged, and what

appeared to be a middle-aged housekeeper in uniform cracked open the door. “Can I help you?”

He held up his badge, saying, “I’m Detective Rainwater from the Farmersville PD. I need to know if the family of Julie Hartness lives here.”

“Mr. Hartness does.”

“Is he in?”

The short, plump woman opened the door wider, hands settling on her hips. The expression in her eyes was about as warm as a snow blizzard. “The mister is in the sauna relaxing and does not wish to be disturbed.”

Is that right? He leaned against the doorframe. “Well, tell him there is another mister with a badge outside his door waiting to talk to him.”

“He will not be happy.”

“I can live with that.”

She sized him up with a stony stare. “You might as well come in.”

He stepped inside, and she shut the door. “I’ll go tell him. You can wait right here.”

He took in the extravagant sight of the foyer which could have doubled as a ballroom, complete with crystal chandeliers and delicate, painted murals all over the ceiling. He sauntered over to a huge photograph on the wall above the mantel of a man and woman. The female smiled prettily, leaning against the guy’s chest, his arms encircling her.

“That’s my Julie,” a voice said from behind.

He glanced back to examine a man in bare feet, a white robe, and wet hair.

“She is beautiful.”

“Was, Detective. She’s been dead for twelve years. Maria said you asked if her family still lives here.”

"Yes. We are investigating a crime, and the suspect drove a car like your wife's. We have a partial license plate match."

"I sold the vehicle about five years ago."

Cole approached him. "To whom?"

"A guy that works for me."

"Can you give me his name?"

"Joseph Brown. He's been an employee of mine for nine years. I highly doubt he is involved in any criminal activity though."

"What kind of work does he do?"

"I flip houses, Detective. He takes care of the renovation. Look, what's your name?"

"Cole Rainwater. I'm a detective with the Farmersville PD."

"Joseph lives here in McKinney. I don't think he travels to Farmersville. You have the wrong man. I trust you can show yourself out."

As the guy walked off, Cole said, "Is he bald with gray eyes, wears army fatigues and dog tags?"

Mr. Hartness paused. When he faced him again, his eyes were curious. "What crimes has this man you're looking for committed?"

"Can you answer my question first?"

"I'd prefer to have my attorney present. Have a good day, Detective."

"I'm afraid by the time that can be arranged, this man who may or may not be your employee would have raped and murdered another victim. He's already killed three people. You should see the one who survived. She's still in the hospital. He almost beat her to death and sexually assaulted her for more than ten hours straight. Then he left her for dead in an abandoned hay barn. And all I'm doing here is asking a few questions. If the person guilty of these godawful crimes happens to be the same one working for you, wouldn't you want to know? You don't strike me as the kind of man who would be okay with that."

"Yes," he blurted out.

Cole stood there staring at him. Not sure which one of his questions he just answered.

"The answer to the question you asked me earlier is yes. He resembles your description."

Holy shit.

"If I showed you a picture, Mr. Hartness, can you verify whether or not it's Joseph?"

The man sighed, shrugging his shoulders. "Well, come on then. I don't have all day."

He took out his phone and searched through texts looking for the sketch Gibbs had sent him. When Cole ran across it, he held it out to the guy.

Mr. Hartness took the device and stared at the drawing. The man's expression changed from doubtful to hesitant. He handed the phone back. "It looks like him, all right."

"He came to work for you nine years ago?"

"Yes. I had just gotten my business off the ground, and he answered an ad I had placed for help wanted. He said he was fresh out of the army and had relocated to Texas. In the move he claimed he'd misplaced his driver's license. Since he had no ID, I couldn't write him a payroll check, so I paid him in cash. I was desperate for help at the time, and Joseph is a hard worker. He shows up every day."

"Did he ever renew his driver's license?"

"I don't know. I never pushed the issue. Like I

said, I needed the help, and he does a good job."

"So you don't know if Joseph Brown is his real name or not?"

"Look, I knew there was something fishy about him. He's a loner, never talks about family. Hasn't had a girlfriend since I met him. I figured it best not to pry."

"Is Joseph still driving your wife's car?" If he was, then there'd be no way his employee could be their guy.

"I don't think so. The last time I saw him, he was driving a blue sports utility vehicle. It didn't look new."

The guy was driving a different vehicle because he set the last one on fire. Cole was sure of it. "I'm going to need his address."

"He's staying in one of my rentals. Eighty-nine Cypress Lane."

"Thank you. If I have more questions, I'll be in touch."

He marched to the truck, hardly believing what just transpired, and how close they might be to catching this bastard. The minute his truck door shut, he put the address into the GPS. It was only five minutes away.

****

Jenna's phone rang as she stepped out of the deli during lunch break. Juggling between keeping the sandwich and drink securely in her hand, she finally managed to free the device from her purse. "Hello."

"What are you doing later tonight?" Barbara asked.

"I'm not sure if Cole has plans."

"You had sex with him, didn't you?"

"What?"

"Don't play dumb."

"It's none of your business."

"You'll eventually tell me anyhow."

"What if I don't?"

"So how was it?"

A thrill shot through her just thinking about it. "Which time?"

Barbara chuckled. "I wish I got half the action you're getting. Was it like old times?"

"I thought it was amazing back then. But now…" She unlocked her car and climbed in.

"He's all grown up."

"And developed a magic touch."

She still found herself reeling from the effects. Jenna's head had been in the clouds all day. After he had gotten through with her last night, there would be no concentrating on anything. Making love with Cole after all this time seemed to heal the wounds she'd been suffering from for so long. It had been a feeling of contentment only he could have provided. His touch did so much more than arouse her. It set things right again, the way they were meant to be between them before tragedy set fate spinning in another direction. Cole Rainwater was Jenna's home, her future, and the life she'd been denied all these years. It had never been so clear as it was last night. Coming back to Texas was the start of it.

"Tell Prince Charming he can do without you for one night. I haven't seen your daughter, and I'd love to meet her."

"Emily is with my parents."

After a brief pause, Barbara said, "How did Cole react to seeing Amanda again?"

"I think he'd rather walk barefoot through a briar patch than look at her."

"I can sympathize."

"He's dealing with it better than I thought. And he is so good with Emily. She's bonding with him."

"How did he take it when you told him he had a daughter?"

Another call came in as Jenna started her car. She glanced at the number, not recognizing it. "Someone's calling. Let me get back to you."

"Okay, but don't forget about me."

She answered the other line. "Hello."

"I've got your daughter."

A wave of fear rippled through her. "Who is this?" she asked, already knowing the answer.

"Don't play games. I've got her, and if you ever want to see her again, you'll come to the address I'm about to give you."

She broke out in a cold sweat, adrenaline pulsated through her. Dear God, the monster had Emily. She swallowed hard. "How do I know you're telling the truth?"

"I'll put her on the phone."

Within a few seconds, Emily said, "Momma, I'm scared."

"It's okay, Emily. I'm going to come get you."

"No, Momma, he's just gonna hurt you."

"Is that enough proof for you?" the killer asked, coming back to the phone.

"Don't you dare hurt my daughter," Jenna said, tears welling in her eyes. "I'll do whatever you want."

"Good. Write this address down."

She opened the glove box with trembling hands, and as she fumbled around for paper and something to write with, the feeling of panic heightened. *Calm down. You have to be able to focus.*

Finally running across an old, wrinkled envelope, she snatched it out, then spotted a pen in the cupholder. The shaking was so bad, Jenna was afraid her fingers would not cooperate enough to write anything legible. "Give me the address."

"Eighty-nine Cypress Lane in McKinney. Got it?"

She took a deep breath, forcing herself to concentrate, and scribbled the address.

"You've got fifteen minutes to get here. And one other thing. If you tell someone about this conversation, I'll kill the little bitch before anyone can get through the door. You know I'll do it."

Before she could respond, he disconnected the call.

She stared at the phone, fighting the urge to call Cole. There was no doubt the killer planned to murder her. And when he no longer had use of Emily, he'd get rid of the child too.

Before Jenna could talk herself out of it, she dialed his number. It rang a few times. *Oh God, please pick up!* His voicemail came on. Heart in her throat, she tried again, getting the same result.

She put the address into her GPS. It was a good twelve minutes away. If she called the McKinney PD, they'd need to be briefed on the situation. They'd never make it in time.

Two minutes had already ticked by, and she needed to come to a decision now before the clock ran out. She pulled her car onto the service road. There was no other choice. She'd have to go it alone to save Emily. If no one showed up in thirteen minutes, he'd execute her without so much as batting an eyelash.

The light turned red as Jenna maneuvered into the turning lane. There was no time to wait it out. She stomped on the accelerator, praying to God the intersection could be cleared safely.

Through the passenger's window, the sight of the station wagon barreling down on her sent her heart to her feet. Too late she realized she'd made a terrible mistake. Before the brakes could be applied, the vehicle plowed into the rental car, forcing her across the road.

Something crashed into the driver's side and her head slammed against the window.

****

Cole's phone rang. It was Gibbs. Cole said, "I was just about to call you."

"Where are you?"

"You know the last name on the list of registered car owners, Julie Hartness?"

"What about her?"

"We hit paydirt, man. Her husband still lives there. And the guy who works for him matches the description from our sketch."

"You're kidding me?"

"He's been an employee for nine years and came straight out of the army. The husband sold his wife's car to this guy a few years ago. But he's not driving it anymore. He's getting around in a blue sports utility vehicle."

"Because he burned the other car to throw us off his trail. But what happened to the dead man's car he stole?"

"I'm sure he ditched it. He had to have known once we found the victim that would lead us to the type of car he drove."

"But he switched the plates."

"He was buying time. That's all. This asshole isn't

stupid. And he knows we're not either."

"What's his name?"

"Joseph Brown. Hartness claims the guy had lost his driver's license when he applied for the job. I'd wager that's not his real name."

"You on your way there now?"

"I'm only a few minutes away," he said, exiting the highway.

"You'll need backup. What's the address?"

"Eighty-nine Cypress Lane, McKinney."

"I'll put a call into the PD out there. They can get there a lot quicker than us." After a pause, Gibbs said, "Hey, Cole. There was a bomb threat reported at the inn. Did you hear about it?"

"What are you talking about?" Surely it couldn't be the same hotel his daughter was staying at. "Which inn?"

"Where Emily and her grandparents are."

"You're full of shit, Gibbs."

"I wish I was, brother."

He didn't like the sound of his partner's voice. "Tell me you have my daughter."

"She got lost in the crowd as they were evacuating and we haven't been able to locate her. That's why I called you."

Panic gripped him. "How in the hell could you guys let that happen?"

"If I would have been there, it wouldn't have."

"By the time I get through with Reed," he said, referring to the officer assigned to stand guard over Emily, "he'll be lucky to still walk."

"We're going to find her, Cole."

The truth was, he was angrier at himself than any

of them for allowing this to happen. He should have always kept that little girl near him. Letting her out of his sight for even a minute turned out to be a tragic mistake. What if something happened to her? No, screw that. Not on his watch. He'd move heaven and earth to keep that from occurring. "That son of a bitch has my daughter, and I'm going to get her back."

"Wait for backup. Channing's calling them now."

He glanced at the GPS, realized his destination was less than a quarter mile ahead, and slowed down. "Does Jenna know?"

"We just got word. You were the first call I made."

Cole pulled the truck over. Gazing out the window, he realized he was in a residential neighborhood with several houses under construction. House number eighty-nine was only two blocks away, within walking distance. "Before you call and alarm her, give me a chance to handle this."

"You're already there, aren't you?" his partner asked flatly.

He slipped out of his vehicle, shutting the door softly behind him, and slid the Glock 22 from its holder. Cole snatched the phone away but could still hear Gibbs' warning in the background, "Dammit, Cole, don't go in there alone. Backup will be there in about fifteen minutes."

He crept forward, catching a glimpse of the back of a blue sports utility vehicle sitting in the driveway. This was the place, all right.

"Do you hear me, Cole?"

He placed the phone back against his ear. "Sorry, buddy. But she could be dead in fifteen minutes. I'm going in."

"Don't be stupid. Just wait."

He disconnected the call and turned his phone off, not wanting to risk it ringing while he was sneaking up on this bastard.

"Don't worry, Emily. Daddy's coming for you," he whispered, as he stealthily made his way to the rear of the house.

He cased the back door, checking the knob. It wasn't locked. And it wouldn't take a genius to figure out a masterful killer like this guy didn't just leave doors unsecured. Not unless it was done on purpose.

But who was the perp waiting for? It wasn't like he could have known they'd tracked the vehicle down to its original owner on this day and at this exact time. Unless his boss had called and warned the suspect they were coming. But the man didn't strike him as the type to do something like that. If he planned on tipping the guy off, he would have never given authorities the information they needed to catch him.

Even if it was a trap, he needed to get in there to save his daughter. Cole was Emily's only chance right now. And his fear was heightened by the concern it may already be too late. Hastiness is how police got killed every day. But sometimes, it was also how people were saved.

With his mind made up, he turned the knob with one hand and raised the Glock with the other.

Cole entered, but before he could complete a full perimeter sweep, something crashed down on his head.

Chapter Fourteen

"Are you okay, ma'am?"

The words echoed through Jenna's mind as if they were a dream. She struggled to wake up, but the urge to drift back into sleep was just too great.

"C'mon, honey. Pull out of it. I need you to open your eyes."

No, I can't, she heard herself say, strangely aware the words never made it past her lips.

"You're gonna be okay. Help is on the way."

Help. Why do I need help? What happened? Who's talking to me?

Then the terrible pain in her head and legs sliced through her body. Sirens wailed in the distance. They drew closer, and Jenna detected the screeching sound of vehicles stopping, feet running toward her.

The weight of her eyelids was incredibly heavy as she fought to open them. A hazy figure loomed over Jenna. "It's okay." This time it was the voice of a male. "I'm Michael with the fire department. I'm here to help. We're going to get you out of here."

Somewhere in the distance, someone said, "Get on the radio and tell them we need the jaws of life. Like right now."

Those words struck fear in Jenna's heart. Opening her eyes all the way caused a burning sensation to erupt. Everything was blurry. She struggled to sit up.

The man named Michael grabbed her, holding her in place. “Oh, no, honey, don’t move. Just stay still for me, okay.”

“I can’t see,” she said, battling the panic threatening to take control of her.

“Let me help,” he said, wiping her eyes with something soft.

After blinking a few times, her vision cleared. And she gazed up into the brown eyes of the man leaning over her. He smiled reassuringly. “See. It’s okay. It was just a little blood. You cracked your head pretty hard, and it’s bleeding.”

It occurred to her she had been rushing to get somewhere. *Where was I going?* The memory of the phone call with the killer came back with a vengeance. “Emily!” She strained against Michael, pushing him out of the way to get up.

He resisted, gently keeping her there. “You can’t move. Your legs are pinned under the dash. Just relax. We’re trying to get you out.”

She’d had a car accident. The image of the station wagon coming at her resurfaced in Jenna’s mind. It had plowed into the rental car she’d been driving, thrusting it across the road. “My daughter Emily is in danger. You’ve got to save her.”

“Whoa, slow down. You’ve hit your head.”

“No. You don’t understand. That’s where I was going before I got into an accident.”

“I know you’re confused right now and—"

“Listen to me, dammit! You pick up the phone right now and call the Farmersville Police Department. Ask to speak with detective Cole Rainwater. Tell him the killer has our daughter Emily, and she is being held at 89 Cypress Lane here in McKinney. He told me if I didn't get there in fifteen minutes, he was going to murder her."

"Wait a minute." A burly cop standing just outside of the passenger's side door looked at her. "Did you say 89 Cypress Lane?"

"That's where my daughter Emily Rainwater is being held hostage."

Tears welled in Jenna's eyes as she remembered how she had fought to put Cole's last name on Emily's birth certificate. It had been the one thing Amanda Langley wasn't going to take away from her. She'd gotten a strange sense of satisfaction at how angry her mother became after she found out what had been done.

"A call just came in for an abduction at that address a few minutes ago," the cop continued.

Jenna sobbed uncontrollably. Somehow, they knew where Emily was. Thank God. "Please rescue my baby. Don't let her die."

"We're going to get to her, ma'am. Don't worry."

"Not ma'am. Jenna Langley." Her eyelids became heavy again, and unconsciousness was taking hold.

"Stay with me, Jenna," Michael said. "I need you to keep your eyes open."

She couldn't fight it anymore. The darkness closed in. "I'm really cold."

"We've got to get her out now. She's losing too much blood." Those words echoed in Jenna's mind before unconsciousness took her.

****

The sound of grunting awakened him. Cole opened his eyes, and Emily came into view seated across the table from him. Duct tape covered her mouth, and she appeared to be tied to a chair as she wiggled—muffled noises coming from her—and he realized her grunting must have roused him from his unconscious state.

He lunged forward, only to be jerked back in place by what must have been the same type of bonds Emily was constrained with. "It's going to be okay, honey," he assured her, even though, given the situation, Cole was not in the least convinced of that.

Her long hair was disheveled and damp with sweat. The child's eyes were wide with fear. Tears streaked down her face. And he'd do anything to take his daughter into a protective embrace, whisk the girl away from this place, and make her feel safe again. Do what fathers do. Protect their children.

Wiggling, Cole noticed the chair he was chained to wouldn't budge. He peered down to see what anchored the legs of the furniture to the ground, but his head snapped back up when Emily grunted again. Her gaze fearfully locked onto something behind him. Footsteps echoed in the distance, coming closer, and Cole's attention traveled in that direction.

"Well, that didn't take long. What were you out," their captor said, coming into view and glancing at his watch, "four minutes?"

Every ounce of anger Cole had been experiencing up to this point evolved into utter shock when the face of the monster he'd been chasing for weeks now stared at him, grinning with delight. "Dad?"

Although the perp resembled his father, he never would have guessed that was the identity of this man. But it couldn't be. Derek Rainwater died in a fire ten years ago.

"I know what you're thinking, Cole. But I'm not

the person I appear to be."

"I know who you are. You're Derek Rainwater."

The man shook his head. "I'm Joseph Rainwater, Derek's twin brother." He sank into a chair. "He never told you about me, did he?"

"My father didn't have a brother."

"Oh, he did. Our sorry-ass parents gave us up for adoption. Derek found a good home. I wasn't so lucky. They shuffled me around from one foster family to another."

"You're a liar."

"Look at me, Cole. Do you think it's a coincidence I am the spitting image of the man who raised you? You're smarter than that, son."

"No!" Cole refused to get wrapped up in the lies of this psychopath. "I don't believe you. I'm not sure how you pulled off a fake suicide, but—"

"Listen to me."

He sat there, stunned.

"Do you remember all those times Derek used to tell you he was going out to visit an army buddy? He was coming to see me while I was locked up in that damn looney bin. You were only a toddler when they came for me. Your good-for-nothing mother ran off. She couldn't handle the pressure of raising a kid by herself. So, I turned to my brother Derek to take care of you. He was supposed to tell you the truth when I got out. But he thought I was just as crazy as they did. And when the time came, he refused to do what he'd promised to. Tell you I am your father. He insisted you were better off with him."

Cole wanted to deny it to his core, but he recalled there had been many times Derek tried to talk to him. It had been obvious to Cole back then his father had been trying to get something important off his chest. But it never quite made it past the man's lips. Cole always blew it off, figuring if he needed to know badly enough, Derek would eventually tell him.

"I couldn't have raised you anyhow. Not with the kind of life I live. All I wanted him to do was tell you the truth."

"You killed him."

"I didn't have a choice. The police were closing in. That damn witness saw me pick up the girl that night in Derek's van."

"You committed your crimes in my father's van?"

He slammed his fist on the table, and Emily jumped. After a few seconds, the man amazingly composed himself. "He is *not* your father. I am! You see the damage he did by not telling you?"

"Why did you use his van?"

"Because I didn't have a vehicle. I broke into his house many times when he was sleeping. I knew where he kept the keys."

"How many times did you break into our house?"

"Enough to know your routine. My brother tried to keep you from me. You are my son, and I had a right to know about your life. And you had a right to the truth. He stole that from both of us, don't you see?"

"Was it worth killing him over?"

"It was either Derek or me. I couldn't get locked up for the rest of my life. I would never have done it if it hadn't come down to that."

"You blame him for not telling me. But you didn't either and you knew."

He shook his head, standing, and pacing the floor.

"It isn't that easy."

"Do you think it was easy for him?"

"Look, it was his responsibility to tell you. He gave me his word."

"He tried, several times. But he never found the courage to see it through."

Joseph came into Cole's view once again, appearing dazed by what he'd told him. "I didn't know that."

"Would it have changed Derek's fate?"

Anger brewed in Joseph's eyes. "You ask too many questions."

"Well, now that you have me and your granddaughter here, what are you going to do?"

"It wasn't supposed to be this way. I took Emily to lure Jenna here. She was supposed to be sitting there, not you."

"So you planned to kill her, just like you tried to do when you broke into her house."

"She's been your downfall all along. You're just too blind to see it. I saw you crying over that bitch when she left you. I'd have hoped you'd have wised up by now and gotten over her. She's just as selfish as your mother. And she kept intruding in my life with her visions. I saw her on the news, going to the police station, trying to tell them what she saw me doing."

Anger coursed through Cole at the way Joseph was portraying Jenna. "You don't get to talk about her that way. How many nights did you come into my room?"

"Why are you still defending her? All she ever brought you is pain. If she'd have come here today, I would have been doing you a favor by taking her out of your life for good."

"Are you going to kill me and your granddaughter?"

"That wasn't the plan."

"What about now?"

"I don't know! Just stop talking!" Joseph smacked a palm against his head as if waging a war with himself.

Cole realized how unhinged the man was becoming. He needed to calm him down. His and his daughter's life depended on it. "Listen, let Emily go; I'll stay in her place. I'll go with you wherever you want. We'll be together as father and son."

"It's too late for that."

Joseph drew a revolver from the back of his pants just as sirens wailed in the distance.

Heart pounding, Cole stared into his daughter's eyes and told her in as calm a voice as he could, "Emily, honey. I want you to close your eyes. Squeeze them shut as tight as you can. I'm right here with you. It's going to be all right."

Whatever tragedy was about to happen, he wanted to spare Emily from seeing it. Doing that for her may have been the only thing left for him to do.

The child did as he asked. Her little face trembled as she put on a brave front. Then Cole said to Joseph. "Please don't do this…Dad. Don't kill my daughter. I'm begging you."

Playing upon the man's emotions by calling him *Dad*, was the only card left in his hand. It was a Hail Mary pass, and he could only pray to God it worked.

The man smiled as if his earlier outburst never occurred. "They're coming for me, Cole. And I can't let them take me. All I ever wanted was for you to know you are my son. I'm sorry I couldn't be the kind of dad you wanted."

In a move Cole never anticipated, Joseph Rainwater placed the gun to his head and pulled the trigger.

****

Cole sat on pins and needles in the family room of the McKinney Medical Center, waiting for news of Jenna's condition. All that had transpired within the last few hours convinced him his world must be spinning out of control.

It wasn't bad enough he'd barged in to save Emily from someone he never knew existed—who, in another strange twist, turned out to be his father. But when he learned of Jenna's accident and that she had been care-flighted to the hospital, his legs nearly gave out. She and Emily were everything in the world to him, and if fate took either one of them away, there was no doubt he'd lose his own will to keep on living.

But Jenna was fighting for her life right now in the surgery room. He had been told she'd lost a critical amount of blood, and her legs sustained serious injuries in the crash. Cole recalled his actions upon arriving here after being briefed on her condition. He had headed straight to the chapel, hit his knees, and prayed to God Jenna's life would be spared, promising he'd do anything just to be granted this one request.

And now, as he sat on the couch, Emily wrapped in his arms, her head pressed against his chest, Cole was doing everything possible to keep tears from spilling down his cheeks. Putting on a strong front for his little girl was necessary. If he fell apart, where would that leave her? But, God, if it wasn't hard as hell.

He glanced across the room to see Amanda staring

at him. For the first time, the woman gave a sympathetic nod, and then stared at the floor, not moving. Robert sat next to her, arm around his wife, appearing grief-stricken. At that moment Cole realized how hard this must be on them. They love her, too.

"Was that man your daddy?" Emily quietly asked, breaking his train of thought.

"He was my biological father. But he wasn't the man who raised me."

"Was the man who raised you a good guy?"

For the first time in ten years, Cole was comforted by the fact Derek Rainwater had been his father in every sense of the word. Gone was the shame of acknowledging that. He could now reflect on the memories of childhood, having been taught and nurtured by Derek, and have a sense of pride in his upbringing.

"The man who raised me was a good guy."

"I've been praying for Momma," Emily said, in a small voice.

"I know, baby. So have I."

"Do you think the doctors can fix her?"

"I think they will try their very best."

"What if she dies?"

"That won't happen. You want to know why?"

It melted Cole's heart when Emily peered up at him, those eyes that resembled his, as heavy with worry as the weight of the world. He managed a reassuring grin for her sake. "Because your momma is as strong as they come. She's going to fight to get better. She knows you're out here waiting for her."

"And you too, right?"

He nodded. "And me, too."

"Do you love her?"

"With all my heart. I always have."

His daughter smiled, arms wrapping around his waist. "Even when she was in Georgia?"

"Even then."

"Momma's lucky to have you."

A sense of indescribable happiness tugged at his heart. "Not as lucky as I am to have you."

She grinned, squeezing him tighter. "I love you, Daddy."

He had wondered if there ever would come a day when she'd feel comfortable enough to refer to him as her father. But he didn't expect to react with this much emotion. He swallowed hard and hugged her back. "I love you too, sweetheart. You will always be my girl."

She giggled and kissed him on the cheek.

"I think I'm going to get coffee. Do you want a juice?"

Emily nodded, releasing him, and he wandered to the coffee station in the back of the room.

Amanda approached just as Cole grabbed a Styrofoam cup, and she took one for herself. He poured his coffee, adding cream, and stirred it. The woman broke the silence. "All Emily could talk about since she got to the hotel was how much fun she had horse riding. Thank you for making her birthday so special."

"It was my pleasure. We all had a great time."

"I can see how close she is to you."

"That's the job of a father. To love and nurture their children. Emily is a special little girl. And I plan to be there for her every day."

She cleared her throat, her expression serious. "Jenna told me about her decision to move back to

Texas so you can spend more time with Emily."

He searched her face, and she moved her eyes away. "How do you feel about that?"

"I don't care for it. Robert and I won't see nearly as much of them anymore. But I understand why she wants to do it. And I guess I have to let them go. Jenna has her life, and my daughter needs to make decisions based on how she wishes to live it. But it doesn't mean I have to be happy about it."

Cole nodded. "I imagine there will come a day when I will be forced to face the same thing with my daughter's wishes. As parents, we all live on borrowed time with our children. Our job is to raise them and prepare them to face the world. In the end, all we can do is hope we did a good job and let them go."

Amanda shook her head. "And how did you become so smart?"

He grinned, laying the coffee stirrer down. "I was raised by a good father. Now if you'll excuse me, there's a little girl over there who needs her juice."

Cole took his coffee, grabbed a pouch of apple juice from the mini-fridge, and walked away, figuring that was as close as he'd ever come to an acceptance from Amanda Langley. He could live with that.

As soon as he handed the pouch to his daughter, the surgeon trudged into the waiting room. "I'm looking for the family of Jenna Langley."

Robert came to his feet. "How is she, Doctor?"

Cole took Emily's hand, and they walked toward the physician. Amanda sidled up beside them. "She's going to be okay," he said, wiping his brow. "When Jenna came in, she was close to bleeding out. But we were able to get her a blood transfusion quickly enough.

She's got some fractures in the lower leg as well as her femur, that's her thigh bone. You're looking at about a five-month recovery time for that. What concerned us the most was the severed artery in her heel. That's what caused her to lose so much blood. But through surgery, I was able to reconnect the vessel so, with some vigorous and prolonged PT, she'll regain normal function in her foot and ankle."

"I was told she'd hit her head," Cole said.

He nodded. "We performed a CT scan to check for brain trauma. But there doesn't appear to be any. Remarkably, I don't even think she suffered a concussion. The firefighter on the scene who briefed me said Jenna seemed coherent. At least enough to insist they call a Detective Rainwater to rescue her daughter from an abduction that had taken place. She even remembered the address. Said she had been on her way there when the accident occurred."

Cole remembered seeing missed calls from her when he had gotten his phone turned back on. Jenna must have been trying to reach out to him once she'd received word from the killer that Emily had been taken hostage. Joseph made mention he expected Jenna, not him. But Cole had already been at the guy's house and turned off his phone so he wouldn't alarm the kidnapper as he made his approach.

When there had been no answer, Jenna must have decided to go it alone for the sake of saving Emily. If his phone would have been on, and he'd responded when she called, the accident would have never happened. *Stop it.* Going down that rabbit hole right now would only cause more misery and he was far too distraught. "Can we see her?"

"She's been through a long surgery and is still pretty out of it. But I'll let two people go in for ten minutes."

Cole got the shock of his life when Amanda spoke up. "Cole and Emily should go."

He stared back at her. "Are you sure?"

At Amanda's nod, Robert said, "She's right. It should be you two."

"C'mon, Daddy," Emily insisted. "Let's go tell Momma we love her."

Cole kissed the top of his daughter's head, took her by the hand, and walked with her down the hall.

Upon arriving to the room, they slowly opened the door and stepped into the soft darkness.

Jenna appeared so small lying there sleeping under the white thermal blanket. A gauze bandage was taped to the right side of her forehead, marking the spot where he knew she must have hit her head in the accident. The closer he got, the more visible additional minor injuries became. A bruise the size of a quarter marred her cheek, and when he leaned over her and picked up her hand, he noticed a few scratch marks on her arm. He gently kissed the tiny one on her wrist and brushed a stray lock of hair away from her pale face.

His heart bled to see her in this wounded state. And he wished more than anything that he could trade places with her. Taking on her suffering would be done without a thought. That's how deep his love was for this woman. A tear rolled down his cheek.

"Daddy," Emily whispered, her tiny voice was like an angel calling out to him in his grief.

He looked at her. "Yes, baby?"

"Momma's gonna be okay."

The child did her best to give him a reassuring smile. But in her eyes, he caught the hint of burden no child should have. She was putting on a brave front for his sake.

Profound love for his daughter swept over him in that moment. Although she was worried about her mother, she wanted to ease his pain. “Come here,” he said, holding open his arm.

The moment she came to him, he held her close. “We’re all going to get through this, sweetheart. Daddy’s just a little upset to see her this way.”

“I know,” she said, her small voice cracking on a sob. She clung to him.

And he wrapped both arms around her. This was his family. He and his daughter would lean on each other. They would be strong for Jenna.

A nurse quietly stepped into the room, signaling the end of their visit.

Cole nodded, kissed Jenna on the cheek, and turned toward the door. “C’mon, honey,” he said to Emily. “Let’s go home and give Momma some time to rest.”

“Is it okay if I stay with you tonight, Daddy?”

“I wouldn’t have it any other way.”

****

Cole blinked in the morning light that shined through his bedroom window. He sat up in bed and rubbed his eyes. According to the digital clock on the bedside table, it was nine a.m. He recalled not slipping off to sleep until three in the morning. Once he had arrived home last night, Emily was fast asleep in the backseat. He carried her to the guest bedroom and tucked her into bed. But once he walked to his room, and stripped off his clothes, climbing into the bed himself, he had been too sick with worry to fall asleep. He tossed and turned until exhaustion finally won out.

Now, he needed to get a move on. He wanted to get to the hospital to check on Jenna as soon as possible.

His phone rang, and he grabbed it off the nightstand. Amanda Langley was calling. "Hello."

"Good morning, Cole. How is Emily?"

He yawned, opening his eyes all the way. "She's good. When we got here last night, she was already asleep. Poor kid was exhausted."

"Did you manage to get some sleep yourself?"

"Not much. But I'll live."

"We didn't get too much sleep last night either."

"Any word on Jenna?"

He remembered leaving his number at the nurse's station last night, insisting they call him if there was any change in her condition. Amanda also promised she'd call him if she found out anything before he did.

"Robert and I have been to see her this morning. She's still not alert. But the doctor came in while we were there, and he thinks she will make a full recovery. It's just going to take a little time."

Cole breathed a sigh of relief. "I'm about to wake Emily, and we are going to head up there."

"About that. I was wondering if it would be okay for us to take Emily to breakfast. Perhaps get her mind off what's going on with Jenna even if it's just for a little while."

Cole frowned, thinking it was a good idea. "She'd probably like that."

"You're welcome to join us if you'd like."

"Thanks for the invitation. But I'm going to check on Jenna."

"I figured as much. Even though she's not responding, we were hoping she'd be able to hear us. Know we're there supporting her."

He couldn't control the weakness in his voice when he said, "That's all we can do. God, I wish we could do more."

A sigh, and then, "She's going to pull through this, Cole. She has to."

A tear fell from his eye again. He wiped it away and cleared his throat. Emily was sleeping in the next room. He needed to stay strong for her. "I pray that you're right."

"We'll be there to pick Emily up in half an hour and drop her by the hospital after breakfast if that's all right. I know she'll kick up a fuss if we keep her away too long. She'll be worried about her mom."

"Sounds good. I'll see you then."

He got off the phone and set it on the nightstand, mind consumed with thoughts of Jenna. The urge to go see her wouldn't let him rest last night. If they would have allowed him, he would have spent the night in her hospital room, right there, in a chair close to her bed. But he'd had Emily to take care of. And he couldn't put her through a sleepless night at the hospital. He had called Gibbs last night, updated him on Jenna's condition, and told him he would not be in today.

Now he crawled out of bed with a heavy heart and reached for the clothes he'd slipped out of last night, pulling them over his body. It was time to wake Emily. Then he'd jump in the shower and make his way to the hospital.

****

Cole drew up a chair beside Jenna's sleeping form,

lifted her hand to his lips, and kissed it. "Hey, baby," he said, an emotional crack in his voice. "The doctor said you're going to be okay."

Now that he was finally alone with her, the turmoil he'd faced since discovering she had been rushed to the hospital in critical condition came rapping at the door of his heart. Tears streamed down his face, and Cole wept in a way he'd not done since the day she left.

When he got control of himself, he confessed, "I remember the first day I met you. You and Barbara were at the rodeo, and you stood in front of me at the concession stand. I purposely bumped into you, just so you'd turn and look at me. And when I saw your face, I thought you were the most beautiful girl I'd ever laid eyes on. From that moment I knew I had to make you mine. And something told me when I did, nothing would ever be the same.

"You brought meaning to my life and made me strive to be better. Then the years went by, and I got comfortable. I took for granted I'd always have you. But when you left, it all came crashing down. I realized without you, my hopes and dreams for the future, my aspirations in life meant nothing if I didn't have you to share them with."

He took a deep breath, sniffling. "You came back to Texas, and even though I was angry because you left, I had hope again. And last night, I was so scared to think I could lose you for the second time."

He drew a small, velvet box out of his jacket pocket, cradling it, and said, "I bought you this ring. I made dinner reservations. I had plans to ask you to marry me last night. I love you, Jenna Langley, with every beat of my heart. And nothing would make me happier than to spend the rest of my life growing old with you."

"Daddy."

He turned to see Emily standing just inside the door. The child appeared distraught. "Why are you crying? What happened to Momma?"

He sniffled again, straightening up. He laid the velvet box on the bedside table and dried his eyes. "No, honey, she's fine. I was just talking to her."

"Oh." She stepped over to the bed, and sat down on the mattress, at her mom's feet.

"How was breakfast?"

She stared at him, concerned. "You sure nothing's happened to Momma?"

The last thing he wanted his daughter to see was him breaking down. And now the girl took it as an indication something bad happened to her mother. "Emily, the doctor expects your mom to recuperate from this. We just have to give her a little time."

"Then why were you crying?"

"I just miss her."

"Are you worried she won't wake up? You can be honest, Daddy."

Her words reminded him of the discussion they'd had after she found out he was her father, when she had concluded telling the truth was always the right thing to do. Looking at her, he couldn't ignore the maturity that emanated from those eyes that so much resembled his own. She wasn't an impractical child. And he could tell she understood the gravity of the situation. He sighed and said, "A little. But a part of me feels that's an unreasonable fear."

She nodded, appearing beyond her years when she

said, “It’s kind of like when you think of all the what-ifs.”

He couldn’t control the grin that sprouted out from the depths of the despair he had been going through. “That’s exactly what it’s like.”

She reached over and patted his leg. “I know those thoughts are scary. But don’t worry. It’s just your mind tricking you.”

“How did you get to be so smart?”

She shrugged, back to being a kid again, then pointed to the black box sitting on the table next to the hospital bed. “What’s that?”

Before he could reach for it, she was off the bed, and had it in her grasp. When she opened it, her mouth formed an O. Then she peered over at him, delight on her little face. “Is this for Momma? Did you ask her to marry you?”

He nodded with a lopsided grin.

“Holy crap!” She handed him the box with a smile that was animated enough to leap from her face and do a little jig across the room. But before he knew it, she was back to being serious again, as she instructed him to put the ring someplace safe, so he wouldn’t lose it when Momma woke up.

“Yes, ma’am.”

“We’re gonna be a family,” she said, jumping in her father’s lap and hugging his neck.

As he held his daughter, Cole realized, with a heavy heart, the only one missing from this happy moment was Jenna. *Wake up, baby. Come back to me. Come back to us.*

****

Cole was certain he was caught up in a bad episode

of *The Twilight Zone*. The last three days were a haze, and he didn't know if he was coming or going. He did a lot of both, between spending as much time as possible at the hospital with Jenna, who had yet to wake, taking his daughter back and forth from his house to the Langleys' hotel room, and putting time in at work. The little amount of sleep he had been getting, worrying about Jenna, did not make up for the energy he had lost during the daylight hours and half of the night.

He slogged down the hallway of the hospital, a bouquet of roses in his hand, hoping today would be the day she'd open her eyes. But it hadn't happened yet. And the possibility that her condition would take a turn for the worse, despite the doctor insisting she ought to make a full recovery, was wearing on him. He had begun to think the hospital staff were not leveling with him. Maybe things had not panned out the way they thought they should have, and they didn't have the heart to tell him the truth.

But as soon as he turned the corner to her room, there was a commotion stirring right in front of her door. Emily was positioned with her back to him. A nurse stood outside talking to the Langleys. Amanda looked on with a numb expression, while Robert spoke with irritation, waving his hands about.

The nurse behind the reception desk quickly moved from around it the moment he locked eyes with her. She rushed toward him and he dropped the roses, fear swinging a mighty blow to his gut. "What happened?" he asked, picking up the pace, heart in his throat.

She blocked his path, putting her arms against him. "Just slow down. Everything's okay. She's awake."

He stopped and closed his eyes, as his pulse

pounded in his ears. “Thank God,” he said on a breathless note. He wanted to drop to his knees and thank the heavens.

“Yes. She opened her eyes about ten minutes ago. She’s been going on about how she has your answer.”

“My answer?”

“I guess you don’t know what that means.”

“No. I don’t.”

“She may be a little out of it. It’s not unusual. The doctor is in there with her right now. We’ll have to wait until he comes out.”

“Ma’am, I’m going into that room,” he insisted, pointing ahead. “If you intend to stop me, you’ll need to call in the army, the marines, and the navy. Catch my drift?”

She stared at him for a moment, until her eyes told him she knew he meant business. She stepped aside.

As he approached, his daughter, who turned and spotted him, came running toward him. “Daddy, Daddy, Momma’s awake.”

“I know, honey.”

“Grandpa’s upset. They won’t let us in to see her.”

“We’ll see about that,” he said, taking his daughter by the hand and marching the few more steps to her door.

He swept past the nurse arguing with the Langleys and put his hand on the doorknob.

The plump nurse turned on him swiftly. “Sir, you can’t…Sir—”

He went through the door with Emily, and footfalls followed in his wake.

“I tried to stop him,” the nurse explained as the doctor looked up at them.

Cole stared past the doctor, to see Jenna's beautiful blue eyes looking at him. "Hey, you," he said, walking slowly toward her. "I brought you roses, but they're all over the floor out there." He glanced in that direction. When he turned his attention back toward her, she was smiling. "It's okay. Maybe some other time."

He was by her side and taking her hand. "How are you feeling?"

"Oh, you know, like I've been in a car accident."

Cole chuckled, and the doctor cleared his throat, saying, "I'll give you guys ten minutes, and then it's back to my examination."

When the doctor cleared the room, Emily said, "I'm gonna go check on Grandma and Grandpa." She rose on her tippy-toes and whispered into her father's ear, "You didn't lose the ring, did you?"

He shook his head.

"I think now is a good time to give it to her." Then she walked toward the door and slipped out.

Jenna smirked with amusement. "What was that all about?"

He scratched his head, dancing around her question. "The nurse said you had my answer."

"Yes."

"We'll what is it?"

She sighed. "I just told you. It's yes."

He furrowed his brows. "What was the question?"

"You don't remember proposing to me?"

He was surprised. "You heard that?"

"Every word."

"So, you're saying yes to my proposal?"

Yes. I love you and I will marry you, Cole Rainwater. Now, can I see that ring?"

He slipped the ring from the pocket of his jeans, took Jenna's left hand and slid it on her finger.

She held it up admiring it in the flashing sunlight. "It's beautiful."

"Not nearly as beautiful as you." He leaned over, gently taking her lips. As the kiss deepened, the heart monitor beeped loudly, interrupting them. "Why, Ms. Langley, I do believe your heart rate just went up."

The nurse who stopped him in the hallway earlier, rushed into the room. He made quick work of moving away from her, sitting down, and doing his best not to appear the guilty one.

The nurse's attention traveled to Jenna, then suspiciously to him. He cleared his throat as the woman stepped over to the monitor, silencing it. "Are you upsetting my patient?"

"No."

"Then what were you doing?"

He glanced at Jenna for assistance. She just lay there not saying anything.

Well, she's about as helpful as a heart attack.

The nurse put her hands on her hips, impatiently awaiting his response.

He cleared his throat again, peering down. "I was kissing her."

"Oh."

Jenna perked up. "He proposed to me."

Nice that she finally decided to chime in. Cole figured he ought to get used to it, or he'd be ill-prepared to spend the rest of his life with this woman who always seemed to do what she wanted when she wanted.

"Well, congratulations." Then she shook her head

disapprovingly, wagging a finger at him. "But you need to stop getting her excited. There'll be plenty of time for that later."

"Yes, ma'am."

She winked at Jenna and strolled out of the room.

Cole picked up the hand he placed the ring on, and put every finger to his lips, taking his sweet time, kissing each one, the same way he had done the last time they made love.

The heart monitor beeped again, and he groaned. "You realize they're going to have to throw me out of here."

"Will you come back to me?"

"Every day for the rest of my life."

A word about the author…

Although not a native Texan, Donnette Smith has spent more than half her life living in the Lone Star State. She is an entrepreneur and former business owner of Tailor Maid Services LLC. After spending a few years working as a journalist for the *Blue Ridge Tribune*, she realized her love for writing romantic detective novels. Her stories cover a wide range of genres, from horror, time travel, mystery, fantasy, paranormal, and thriller. But one theme stays the same, there is always a detective solving a crime, and a gorgeous victim he would lay down his life to protect. Donnette's biggest fascination is with forensic science and crime scene investigations. Her first mystery/suspense novel, *Lady Gabriella*, was published in 2008. Her second novel was a horror/mystery/suspense titled *Cunja* and debuted in 2012. Her newest novel, *Killing Dreams*, is a fantasy story and is soon to be released.

Donette loves to hear from her readers. Contact her at: www.donnettesmith.com